CASH MONEY CONTENT

MURDERVILLE 3

THE BLACK DAHLIA

FROM THE MINDS OF

ASHLEY & JAQUAVIS

Murderville 3
The Black Dahlia

Copyright © 2013 by Ashley & JaQuavis

Cash Money Content™ and all associated logos are trademarks of Cash Money Content LLC.

First Trade Paperback Edition: September 2013

Book Layout: Peng Olaguera/ISPN

Cover Design: Oddball Dsgn

For further information log onto www.CashMoneyContent.com

Library of Congress Control Number: 2012954025

ISBN: 978-1-936399-09-3 pbk

ISBN: 978-1-936-39910-9 ebook

10 9 8 7 6 5 4 3 2 1

Printed in the United States

MURDERVILLE 3

PREVIOUSLY IN MURDERVILLE 2

LIBERTY SAT OUTSIDE OF PO'S HOUSE AND felt like an outsider. Her castle had been usurped by another woman, and Liberty didn't even feel comfortable enough to knock on the door. She sat in her luxury car a few houses down, lurking, waiting impatiently for Dahlia to leave. Liberty didn't want to run into her. She was too embarrassed, angry, and hurt to even face her right now. Although Po never confirmed that he was fucking Dahlia, Liberty's intuition told her that he had. The average woman would have sought revenge, but Liberty just wanted peace.

The night before had been turbulent, and she had rushed out of the house without thinking. Driving the streets of L.A. all night had given her time to think. She didn't want anything from Po except the original money that they had come upon when they had robbed Samad. She would take her cut and nothing more. He owed her that, but he could keep the rest. She couldn't believe that Po would think she was stealing from him, but she didn't feel the need to explain herself. The relationship had run its course, and Liberty was left heartbroken for the third time in her life. Her first heartbreak had come from watching her father be murdered; the second time had been when A'shai committed suicide in order to join her in death, a death that she had yet to see. Now Po had pushed her out of his life and deserted her when she needed him the most.

Finally, she saw Dahlia's car pull out of Po's estate. She waited a few moments to make sure that the coast was clear before she slid through the gate.

She entered the house and rushed upstairs, moving with haste as she pulled her luggage out from under the bed. She just wanted to get in and out of there as quickly as possible. When she entered the closet, she immediately noticed the rolls of money lying on the floor. She knelt down and flipped through the bills.

This isn't mine. What the fuck? She thought. Liberty picked the money up off the floor, scooped it into a shoe-box, and placed it back on the shelf. *Does he think that I took this from him? This money isn't even worth taking. I have ten times that of my own. Why would I risk our relationship for chump change?* She turned the box to the side and noticed that it was for shoes in a size seven. She saw red as the number jumped out at her, because she wore a size ten. She stormed out of the bedroom and waltzed into Dahlia's room, heading straight for her closet. A shoe whore at heart, Dahlia had a closet lined with boxes and boxes of designer footwear. Liberty read the size on one of them, and sure enough, size seven was on the boxes.

"Ahem!"

The sound of someone clearing her throat caused Liberty to drop the shoebox from her hands. She turned around quickly to see Dahlia standing behind her, arms folded across her chest as she looked at Liberty challengingly.

"I thought Po made himself clear yesterday," Dahlia said. "You need to leave."

"You bitch. You set me up. You planted this money inside my closet so that Po would think I was stealing from him!" Liberty accused.

"So you know," Dahlia said with a shoulder shrug. "What are you going to do about it, Liberty?"

Dahlia walked toward Liberty and began to walk around her, circling her as she spoke. "You gonna tell him? You gonna force me to leave and reclaim your throne?" Dahlia was so close to Liberty that the scent of her perfume made Liberty's stomach churn in disgust. "You have no idea who you're fucking with. I already took your man, dear cousin. Don't make me take your life. Your best bet is to stay out of my way before I put you in the dirt the same way I did Omega," Dahlia threatened.

Liberty's eyes widened in surprise. She couldn't believe that Dahlia had murdered Omega. She brushed past her cousin, realizing that she never really knew her. This could not be the same little girl she played with, bathed with, and slept with as a child. Dahlia was the devil's seed. Disgusted, Liberty quickly grabbed the key to her safe-deposit box and rushed out of the house. A part of her wanted to call Po and warn him about who he was dealing with, but the other part said fuck it. He had chosen Dahlia, and there was nothing he could ever say to take away the painful sting of that decision. *He has no idea who he has invited into his bed*, she thought as she reached her car. This time, she refused to go back.

Just as Liberty was getting into her car, she saw Rocko walking up to the house.

"Rocko! Where's Po? I need to see him," she said in frustration and pain.

"I don't know. We just got back to the States this morning. He had to go handle some other business," he said as he noticed the pained look on her face. "Why? Is everything OK?" he asked.

"It's nothing," Liberty said as she turned her head, trying to disguise her true feelings.

Rocko gently grabbed her by the shoulders and looked into her eyes. "What's wrong? You look crazy right now," he asked, knowing that Liberty wasn't being completely honest with him.

"Po is not the same, Rocko. That bitch is controlling his mind and fucking up my life," Liberty said as her voice began to crack. She felt her knees begin to buckle, and Rocko held her up and hugged her.

"Whoa, I got you, Liberty," he said as he held her up. "Don't worry about it. I'm going to have a talk with Po. He's too smart to let this bullshit take place. I feel it in my heart that something isn't right with Dahlia. She has evil eyes. She has a bad soul." Rocko looked toward the house and saw Dahlia standing in the window looking down on them with an evil stare.

Dahlia watched as Rocko embraced Liberty. She smiled devilishly as she stepped back from the window and began to put her plan into motion. "So, you're the next one to go, huh?" Dahlia said to herself as she saw that Rocko had picked sides. *Too bad, I actually liked you, Rocko,* she thought as she folded her arms and watched them from afar. In her twisted mind, anybody who stood next to her enemy would be caught in her crosshairs. Therefore, Rocko had to get forced out of the picture, too.

Dahlia was becoming addicted to power. She loved that she had one of the most powerful men in the drug game under her thumb. She understood that pillow talk controlled the world, and when you are pillow-talking with a boss, you run his world. She was meticulously establishing her position of power and was at the point of no return. Omega had kept her dormant for so many years, but now, with him out of the way, she was transforming into what she was meant to be: the Queen Bee.

Rocko looked up at her, and they locked eyes. It seemed as if the beamed laser of Rocko's nasty stare shot directly to Dahlia. She smiled sinisterly and turned away. She knew at that moment that Rocko was her enemy and a potential wedge between her and Po. She had to do something about that situation. She peeked out once again and watched as Rocko and Liberty got into their cars and pulled off. She thought it was odd that Rocko followed Liberty in his car as she pulled away, so she quickly grabbed her keys and rushed out. She wanted to see where they were going and what they were doing.

Liberty walked into the hotel room she had been staying in, with Rocko close behind her. They agreed to talk about how to approach Po. They both knew that Dahlia had played a big part in his sudden change of character.

"I have been trying to call him. I want him to meet us here, so we can all talk and get this shit together. We have to keep our core strong and tight, and I don't believe we can do that with this bitch Dahlia in the picture," Rocko preached as he stood by the door, attempting to call Po again.

"I'm glad you noticed it, too. Something's not right with her. She is crazy, and she has Po moving very sloppy," Liberty added.

"Everything is going to be smooth. I just have to pull my man's coattail on this one. Po is a gangster, and he's going to step back and respect it. He'll make everything right. Trust me. I just can't get in contact with him. His line is going straight to voice mail."

Dahlia quickly drove back to the house as she began to put her plan together in her head. She smiled, seeing that she had beat Po home. He had a meeting with a coke connect earlier that day, and she expected him any minute now. She quickly rushed into the house with her camera in hand. She had taken photos of Liberty and Rocko entering the hotel room just minutes ago, and she knew how she could work it in her favor.

She walked past the hall mirror. It seemed as if her reflection made her stop in her tracks. She looked at herself. She looked into her deep brown eyes and glanced at her cocoa skin. A smile formed on her face, and she didn't know why. As she looked deeper, she finally realized that she was smiling. She actually liked being conniving and deceitful. It gave her a rush, and it was becoming a slight obsession. She had always been attracted to powerful men, but she was coming to realize that it wasn't an attraction; instead, it was a desire to be in their position. She hurried to the bedroom so that she could prepare for Po's arrival.

Po pulled into his driveway and took a deep breath. He'd had a long week and just wanted to lie back and relax. The thought of Liberty filled his mind, but when he started to think about how she had deceived him, rage overpowered the love. He approached the door, and Dahlia stood in the doorway waiting for him . . . naked. The only thing she wore was black lipstick and black six-inch heels. Her fat vagina seemed to be sitting up, and it was shaven bald, so Po could see every crease. His eyes scanned her body as he approached the door. He was speechless. His manhood instantly began to rise as she opened the screen door and grabbed him by his belt buckle.

Dahlia pulled him in as she walked backward. His hands instantly gripped her perky breasts, and he began to massage them. A small moan escaped her lips as she closed her eyes and ran her tongue across her top lip. Once Po got completely into the house, she dropped to her knees and unbuckled his pants. She quickly pulled Po's rock-hard tool from his jeans and took him into her mouth. She was about to put down another plot, but first, she needed to have Po in his weakest state. She, being a master manipulator, knew that weakness came after a man had been well sexed.

She dropped his pants and began sucking him off as she grabbed his sack with eager hands and began massaging it gently, all while deep-throating him. His phone began to ring. Using one hand, she grabbed the phone, still giving him head, and turned it off. She was doing what she did so well that Po threw his head back and was in a sexual trance. He felt an orgasm fast approaching, and his legs stiffened up as he gripped the back of Dahlia's head, forcing his length deep inside her throat. Dahlia quickly stopped and stood up.

"What's wrong? Why did you stop?" Po asked as he frowned in disappointment. He pipe was sticking straight out, with veins forming all through it. He was just about ready to explode before he was cut short.

She turned around and headed toward the stairs. She smiled, knowing that Po's eyes were on her juicy, round, black assets. She swished harder, making her cheeks jiggle with each step. Just as expected, he followed her up the stairs.

After she sexed his brains out, she would plant the seeds to make her the new Queen Pin and X out everyone who could stop that. She had to separate Po from Rocko and Liberty, and that's exactly what she planned on doing. This was only the beginning of the takeover, a takeover for the ages. Heads were about to roll, and Dahlia would be at the forefront orchestrating it.

An hour later, Po was lying on the bed, breathing heavily, watching the ceiling fan slowly spin around and around. Dahlia had just put the best sex known to mankind on him, and he was basking in the aftermath. As Dahlia, completely naked, walked from the bathroom and joined Po in the bed, she placed a camera on his chest.

"What's this?" Po asked as he looked down at the gadget.

"Just take a look at it, my king. You know I always look out for my man, right? I saw some things that maybe you were too busy to see, and I wanted to put you on to it," she said as she lay beside him and lovingly stroked his limp pole while talking to him.

Po slowly picked up the camera and began to click through the pictures. Dahlia had snapped pictures of Liberty and Rocko entering a hotel room, putting her plan down precisely.

"What is this supposed to mean?" Po asked as he gently tossed the camera onto the bed as if it didn't matter to him.

"I just thought you should know. I thought Rocko was your brethren. He shouldn't be stepping out with your ex, should he?" she asked. She smiled on the inside but had a concerned look plastered on her face.

"Look, ma, I could care less. Rocko is my man, a hundred grand. We don't trip over a piece of pussy, believe that," he stated as he closed his eyes and leaned his head back. Although he didn't show it to Dahlia, he was steaming on the inside. He didn't want to show his real feelings to her, but his clenched jaws told it all.

Dahlia smiled as she grabbed the vial of coke from the nightstand and placed a small pile between her thumb and fingers. She took a bump and then prepared one for Po. He quickly snorted the coke off her hand and rested his head on the bed. He smiled as his rod instantly began to grow. He had discovered that sex with coke and Dahlia was the next best thing to heaven. It got to the point where every time they had sex, he had to have coke in his system. What he thought of as having a good time was actually the deceitful web that Dahlia was spinning. She controlled his mind while he was high and horny.

She smiled as she saw the coke taking effect on Po and lowered her head, putting her juicy and warm mouth on his now-growing rod. Her seed had been planted. Now the only thing she would have to do was water it, and Rocko would eventually get pushed out of the circle as she had planned. In her twisted mind, Rocko was on Liberty's side, and that made him her enemy. She knew that to fully control Po's thoughts, she had to separate him from any and every person he loved. Then she would eventually call all the shots . . . through him.

Two weeks had passed, and Po had completely cut Rocko off. He never told him the reason behind their sudden disassociation, but honestly, Po's ego was bruised. Dahlia had consistently drilled into him that Rocko was jealous of him and would eventually come for his spot. She was highly intelligent and had managed to break a bond that was once so strong. With the sex and the drugs, Po had no chance against Dahlia's game of mental chess.

Rocko, on the other end, had been trying to catch up with Po, but his calls went unreturned, and the door was never answered. Po's business in the streets was going unhandled, and Rocko knew something was up. He intuitively knew that Dahlia was behind his man's change of character. He kept in contact with Liberty and checked up on her frequently, trying to be the bridge between her and Po, but with no contact with his man, things didn't look good. He let Liberty borrow his car for the week because her car had been "mysteriously" vandalized, and all her tires had been sliced. She put the car in the shop, and Rocko let her use his tinted Range Rover for the weekend.

Rocko drove on the highway, heading to Po's house, hoping to catch him there. He had to see what the deal was. He had no idea that Dahlia had cunningly turned Po against him. Just the one hug that he gave Liberty, which was seen by Dahlia, had changed their whole relationship.

The sun's beams shone down on the massive blue ocean. There wasn't a cloud in the sky. Po stood on the dock and looked at Dahlia, who stood on the boat, applying suntan lotion to her arms and neck. Her voluptuous body filled out the two-piece Burberry swimsuit nicely. Po looked down at his watch and then slid his hands into his pocket. Dahlia looked over at Po and smiled as the boatmen pulled up the anchor and prepared for their weekend at sea. It was Dahlia's idea to take a weekend getaway, and Po felt it was needed.

He yelled over to Dahlia. "I'll be right back. I have to talk to my man," he said as he walked down the boardwalk toward the parking area. A tinted Range Rover was waiting for him. Po looked around and then got into the vehicle, where Li'l Mikey waited on him.

"What's up, big homey?" Li'l Mikey said as he gripped the steering wheel and checked the rearview mirror.

"What's good, li'l man?" Po asked as he looked over at the live wire from his old trap spot.

"Thanks for copping me this nice-ass whip," Li'l Mikey said as he smiled and rubbed the wood grain on the steering wheel.

"No doubt. That's what you get when you move up in the ranks, li'l homey," Po said as he reached into his pocket and pulled out a small vial of coke. He emptied a small pile onto the dashboard and then used his nose as a vacuum to snort it up. He passed the vial to Li'l Mikey, who poured a small amount between his thumb and his finger. He snorted it like a pro and threw his head back to prevent his nose from running.

"I got you. I'ma hold you down," Li'l Mikey said as he nodded his head up and down with a cold stare.

Po really did not trust Li'l Mikey, but he loved his coldness and live-wire attitude. He felt he needed a crazy nigga on his team to take the place of Rocko. The heavy coke snorting began to cloud his judgment, and he began to move sloppy. He didn't realize it, but Dahlia had begun to call the shots.

"Remember what I said. Make it clean and quick." Po stated as he reached into his pocket and pulled out a roll of money. He placed it in Li'l Mikey's lap, and Li'l Mikey's eyes lit up like a Christmas tree.

"I got you! Rocko will be out of here before you get back from your trip. It's a new era," Li'l Mikey said as he wiped his nose and nodded his head up and down.

Li'l Mikey had spotted Rocko's car earlier that day and was just waiting on the confirmation from Po. Po was about to knock off his best friend because of Dahlia's manipulation. She had somehow convinced him that if he didn't get Rocko, Rocko would eventually get him. With the coke in his system, Po was a different person. He was about to commit the ultimate betrayal. He slapped hands with Li'l Mikey and exited the car, heading back to the boat where Dahlia waited. Their voyage was about to begin as someone else's was about to end.

Rocko pulled up to Po's house and hopped out of the car. He tried calling Po's number again, but this time, he got a disconnection message. "What the fuck?" Rocko said to himself as he looked at the phone's screen to see if he had the right number. He was totally in the dark about what was about to unfold. He walked to the front door and noticed that it was slightly ajar.

"Yo, Po!" he yelled as he put his hand on the doorknob.

He slowly pushed the door open and stepped in with caution. "Yo, Po!" he yelled again.

Rocko stopped in his tracks when he saw about ten Africans standing with guns pointed at him. He quickly tried to reach for his gun, but a single shot rang out, hitting him in the knee, causing him to crumble. A tall chocolate man with a model's physique stepped over him. It was Zulu. He had come over to the States to end the burden that was over his shoulders. Dahlia had to die. The itch of killing her was far too difficult to ignore. He had come over for one reason and one reason only. His secret would die with Dahlia, and he wasn't settling for anything less. He wanted Dahlia's head. Zulu looked down and pointed a gun at Rocko's head.

"I'm going to ask you this one time and one time only. Where . . . is . . . Dahlia?"

Sitting in the parking lot of her hotel, Liberty had a heavy heart. She wiped the single tear that dropped from her face as she sat in the truck and rested her head on the steering wheel. She missed Po and wanted things to be normal, but she realized that she would never be able to make things right. She was ready to leave town and Po for good. She was just waiting until her car was repaired, and then she would leave. As she sat in Rocko's tinted Rover, she thought about the current day's date. It was a date that was close to her heart and dear to her soul. It was the anniversary of A'shai's death. She knew that Po would never give her the love that A'shai once had. Maybe that was why she chased love so quickly with Po. She was merely trying to fill a void that A'shai had left with his death.

Liberty was ready for a new beginning, a new life. She took a deep breath and started up the car. She was headed to get a bite to eat. A vehicle pulled alongside her. She didn't even notice the sinister scowl that the young boy had on his face as things unfolded. "I love you always, A'shai," she whispered as she closed her eyes and imagined his face. Liberty never saw it coming.

Li'l Mikey extended his arm out the window, and shots rang out from his gun as he Swiss-cheesed the truck. He thought Rocko was in the truck, but the tint didn't reveal that it was Liberty he was shooting. *Rat tat tat tat tat tat tat . . .*

ONE

"DAHLIA!" LIBERTY CALLED OUT AS HER FEET *pounded the pavement and she panted from exhaustion, winded as she tried to catch up to her cousin. "Dahlia, wait up! You're going too fast!" she screamed, a hint of terror in her voice. Night was falling, and soon the African jungle around her would be pitch-black. Her father had always warned her of the dangers that lay in the wilderness after dark. "You have to respect the way of the land," he would say. "The animals give us a pass in the daylight, but at night, the jungle belongs to them." His cautious words echoed in her head as she tried to keep up with her dearest cousin. More like sisters, she and Dahlia were inseparable, but Dahlia had the more adventurous spirit. While Liberty had not thought it wise to venture into the jungle for a game of hide and seek, the hint of danger enticed Dahlia, making the mischievous little girl want to do it more.*

"Come on, don't be such a baby, Liberty! Nothing's going

to happen! We'll be out of the jungle way before the sun sets," she had urged.

Liberty had allowed Dahlia to persuade her against her better judgment, only to be surrounded now by nothing but wilderness. Her heart pumped anxiously inside her small chest as fear caused her adrenaline to rise. The sun's light dimmed with each fleeting moment. The orange rays gave way to dusk as the jungle darkened before her eyes.

"Dahlia! Dahlia!" Liberty cried. Her young eyes darted to and fro, searching frantically as fear crept into her heart. Dahlia's ebony skin was hard to detect against the blackness that came with nightfall. Her skin was the perfect camouflage as she hid in the dark shadows of night. Liberty stopped running, resting her hands against her knees as she gulped in air, catching her breath. Suddenly, it seemed as though the sounds around her intensified.

She could hear the hungry growls of wild cats, the threatening hisses of poisonous snakes, and the rustling of leaves as predators maneuvered around her. She shook as her head whipped left, then right, as she tried to adjust her eyes to see the animals around her. She felt like the fallow deer that the men in her village would hunt. She was open, defenseless, and full of fear as her wide eyes misted with tears. She wanted to call out to Dahlia once more, but she seemed to have lost her voice the moment she lost the sunlight. She didn't have the courage to scream out into the unknown.

What she didn't know was that Dahlia was close by and was the only predator focused on Liberty that night. She lurked behind the large trunk of a tree, peeking out at Liberty.

Sure, she loved her cousin, and they shared an inexplicable closeness, but as they grew older Dahlia couldn't help but notice the difference in the way people began to treat them. Liberty's exotic complexion among the ebony children in the village garnered much attention. Her beauty was rare, and Liberty was doted on as if she was birthed from royalty. If gifts were given, Liberty's was always better. During mealtimes, Liberty's portions were always more plentiful. Even Dahlia's own mother had begun to praise Liberty's transformation into adolescence. While Liberty was like a rose, her beauty always apparent, Dahlia was like a black orchid. It took a certain amount of maturity to appreciate the beauty she had to offer to the world. In childhood, she couldn't recognize how exquisite the black orchid was. She was too distracted by the growing rosebud by her side. So while Dahlia loved Liberty, a tiny seed of jealousy had been planted and was being watered with each passing day. How easy it would be for Dahlia to let Liberty fall victim to the jungle's nocturnal dangers. Dahlia knew the forest like the back of her hand. She had hunted there with her father before he died of pneumonia years ago. Every day, she would accompany him on his morning hunt. Before the sun came up, they would be in the jungle. He showed her how to adjust her eyesight and see beyond the darkness. "It is the fear of the dark that paralyzes your vision," he had said. She knew this was true, because once she stopped being afraid of the darkness, she could see in it. He taught her to navigate, to survive, and always to be the predator, never the prey. So as she stalked Liberty, she smiled at the fact that she was the better of the two in this moment.

Liberty's soft features wouldn't save her from the jungle. Out here, Dahlia had the upper hand.

She could practically smell the pit of quicksand that Liberty was about to run into. Dahlia smiled as she imagined her pretty cousin sinking into the abyss. The thought of destroying Liberty was ever present in her young mind, but there was not enough hatred built up in her heart for her to follow through just yet. It would take years of separation and building animosity before Dahlia fully turned against Liberty. She watched Liberty inch toward death unknowingly, and just as she was about to be sucked into the sand pit, Dahlia called out to her.

"Liberty!"

Liberty stopped mid-stride and turned toward Dahlia's voice. "Dahlia!" she cried out.

It was so dark that Liberty didn't see Dahlia until she was right in her face. Liberty's tears instantly turned to anger.

"I told you not to leave me! I told you we would be trapped in the dark! Why didn't you stop running when I called you?" Liberty shouted as she pushed Dahlia in frustration.

"I didn't hear you!" Dahlia shouted in her own defense as she pushed Liberty back. "If it wasn't for me, you would be stuck out here. You shouldn't be so weak. Only the strong ones survive. I'm the strong one. Remember that!"

The look in Dahlia's eyes that night sent chills down Liberty's spine, and years later, as she sat behind the dark tint of Rocko's Range Rover, she felt the same chill. The memory from their childhood had Liberty in a daze. Dahlia had always been the strong one, the fearless one, while Liberty was weak. The pecking order between them had been established from early on, which made it easy for Liberty to fall into the role of victim. What once had been a childhood rivalry had transformed into a relentless vendetta between grown women. It didn't matter that they were blood—one of them had to lose. And as Liberty sat thinking, she made a promise to herself that this time, it wasn't going to be her.

"Only the strong survive, dear cousin," she whispered.

Liberty wiped the tears from her eyes. She was tired of sulking and mourning the loss of Po. *If he wants to choose a bitch like Dahlia over me, then I'll let him,* she thought. *I've tried to warn him, but it's clear that he has to be bitten before he realizes he's sharing his bed with a snake.* Liberty took a deep breath and reached into the backseat to grab the Gucci duffel. All of the money to her name was tucked inside. She didn't trust anyone at this point and needed it within eyesight at all times. She never knew when she would have to pick up and leave. When the time came for her to make her exit, she wanted to ensure that she had the means to do so. She turned to exit the car, but before she could push open the door, a car pulled up on her side. It was so close that she didn't have room to open the car door.

"What the fuck? Hey . . ." she protested as she began to roll down her window. But before she could finish her sentence, bullets rang out, shattering the glass window as all hell broke loose.

BOOM! BOOM!
BOOM! BOOM!

Instinct pulled her to the floor of the car, and screams of fear erupted from her gut as she curled up, tightly hugging her knees while covering her ears.

BOOM! BOOM!

Glass rained down on top of her as the car was assaulted with hollow-tips, and smoke from the gunfire filled the air.

"Agh!" she screamed. She had survived many things, but in this moment, she felt in her bones that her life had reached its end. Everything seemed to move in slow motion as she cowered fearfully. Her heart pounded, and her stomach went hollow. Her eyes widened as she anticipated the pain that the bullets would cause. She waited, wondering why her life hadn't flashed before her eyes. She was hoping, praying, to see A'shai's face. She knew that if he came to her in her final moments, then she could follow him into the light. A piece of her hoped that this was her final day. At least then she could leave the pain of mortality and live in a forever peace with her one true love. Liberty closed her eyes.

BOOM! BOOM! BOOM!

"Agh!" She could hear her blood beating in her ears as her heart took an express elevator down into her stomach. Terror-stricken, she sat immobilized by the threat of imminent death. Tears pricked at her eyes and fell down her cheeks.

The door was snatched open, and Liberty looked directly into the eyes of the masked shooter. She had no idea who Li'l Mikey was, but he knew exactly who she was. Po had made it a point to make sure everyone acknowledged his queen. She was too high up in the hierarchy to know all of his li'l niggas, but everyone on the bottom looked up to her. They were well aware of her position. They knew that she was the lady on Po's arm, and her presence in the vehicle startled Li'l Mikey.

Fuck is she doing here? This is Rocko's whip. She not supposed to be here! His thoughts were frantic as he snatched her out of the Range Rover violently, pointing a pistol directly in her face.

"Where's Rocko?" he shouted with a raspy baritone as he gripped her collar with one hand while keeping his aim steady with the other.

"I don't know!" she screamed as she pulled her head back in resistance. "I don't know, I don't know!" She choked on her own sobs as she closed her eyes and waited for the blast that would end her life.

Li'l Mikey was indecisive. In any other circumstance, he would have pulled the trigger, but Po's directions had been clear. He wanted Rocko's head on a platter. Li'l Mikey didn't want to be the one to make the decision to execute wifey. It wasn't his call, so instead of finishing what he had started, he flung Liberty to the ground and ran over to his car. He hopped inside and pulled off recklessly, burning rubber as he made his getaway.

Liberty turned and tried to run, but her legs were like Jell-O. Unstable and trembling, she could barely keep her balance as she grabbed her duffel bag. Patrons and hotel staff had begun to filter out of the hotel.

"Miss are you OK?" a valet worker asked as he ran to assist her.

Liberty shook her head and pushed him off of her slightly. "I have to get out of here," she whispered frantically, speaking more to herself than anyone else.

"The police . . . they are on the way. You really should wait for them . . ."

Liberty pushed through the crowd of onlookers and ran into the middle of the street. She stood directly in front of oncoming traffic, causing a cab to come to a screeching halt in front of her. The cab driver jumped out of the car, enraged.

"Hey, lady! Are you insane?" he asked as he threw up his hands in frustration.

Liberty rushed around the car and hopped inside. "You get me out of here as fast as possible, and I'll give you five hundred dollars," she said.

Without a second thought, the cab driver hopped into the car and pulled away from the chaos. Liberty hunched down in her seat as the sounds of police sirens neared. She reached for her bag and removed her cell. Her first thought was to call Po, but she quickly decided against it. She had to see him face-to-face. She knew that he didn't harbor enough hate for her to put a hit out on her. If she had been the target, she would be circled in chalk right now. *The shooter was coming for Rocko.* She gasped as dread filled her when she came to her next realization. *On Po's order.* The thought caused her much distress, because she knew that although Po was the only one who could order such a hit, it was Dahlia's influence that had caused it to happen. She leaned her elbow on the edge of the window and brought the back of her hand to her forehead as she exhaled. She had to stop this. As much as she wanted just to take her money and run toward the future, she couldn't. Loyal to a fault, she felt obligated to open Po's eyes to Dahlia's manipulative ways. To leave Po in Dahlia's clutches was equivalent to killing him herself. Dahlia was like poison, and she had infected Po. *I have to get him to see clearly, because if he doesn't, she is going to ruin him.*

TWO

"MMM." DAHLIA COULDN'T CONTAIN THE MOAN THAT escaped her slightly parted lips as she watched Po hit the lines of blow that were laid out between her legs. The sun beamed brightly, sending heated rays down upon them as they sat aboard the luxurious yacht that Dahlia had persuaded Po to rent for the weekend. Halfway to Mexico, Dahlia and Po had anchored their vessel to bask in the middle of the ocean. Po lifted his head and gave her a crooked smile as he sniffed and rubbed the cocaine residue from the tip of his nose. Dahlia grinned mischievously. Po was a beautiful specimen of a man. If she were a weaker woman, he would surely have her wrapped around his finger; fortunately for her, she was the puppeteer. She tensed as she felt Po trace a finger up and down her womanhood. The thin fabric of the gold string bikini she wore was soaked immediately from her fountain.

"Damn, you're wet," he whispered, in awe of her. Dahlia

was always wanton and ready. Her sex game was out of this world. She was well versed in pleasing a man. She never said no, and Po loved that about her. The feel of his fingers on her most delicate places caused goose bumps to form on her body. He massaged her pulsating clitoris through the fabric. Dahlia sucked air between her teeth as she rotated her hips slightly, matching his rhythm as he slowly rubbed her pussy.

"This my pussy?" he asked.

Dahlia flashed him a wicked smile as she came up on her elbows so that she could see him better, but she never answered. *No, nigga, this is my shit*, she thought. She was the boss. She was the ruler of her own universe. She knew that if a man owned her body, then he owned her mind. Dahlia wasn't a possession; she was the possessor. When she first laid eyes on Po, she was attracted to his American boy appeal. He walked as if he was capable of taking over the world, he talked with a slight Southern drawl that made her panties moist with every syllable, and he carried a street aura that told her he feared no one. She knew that she had to have him when she saw how he treated Liberty. He was attentive, protective, providing, but still supportive. He gave Liberty the freedom to live, something that Dahlia did not have. Dahlia had lived on a tight leash until she weaseled her way into Po's bed. Now she had the world at her feet as she sat beside Po as his new queen. There was only one problem: being queen wasn't enough for Dahlia. She didn't want to be the woman behind the man. She wanted to be the king, and now Po was in the way.

She sucked her teeth, hissing in pleasure, as he moved her bikini bottom to the side and found her treasure. He licked her lips upward, then downward, upward, then downward, lapping at the folds of her pussy as if they were covered in honey. Her clit swelled in anticipation. She knew that he was purposely avoiding her love button, making her eager as she squirmed at his touch. *This man's head is phenomenal . . . it's such a shame that it's time to get rid of him,* she thought.

"Hurry," she whispered.

"Be patient," he responded as he kissed a trail up her body, moving on to her nipples. He circled his tongue around her mounds, and her body reacted. Her back arched as she pushed her pelvis into the bulge that had formed under his linen pants. She reached down and freed him. She gasped as she felt his skin against her skin. The head of his dick was so full, so thick, and her insides clenched achingly. *Nothing wrong with one last fuck before I ruin his life,* she thought. He parted her legs as he nuzzled her neck and then reached into his pocket to retrieve a condom. He leaned back, opened the wrapper, and rolled it onto his length. The first stroke was always the best. Dahlia felt his thickness open her up, filling her to her limit.

"Ooh," she whispered. Her hands wrapped around his torso as she spread her fingers wide, decorating his back with her long, red, stiletto nails. Po and Dahlia didn't make love. Their sex was carnal. They fucked like animals every time they were intimate, each trying to outdo the other, battling for control. Po's stroke was relentless as he hit her, working his hips with no mercy as he pushed down on her left thigh while holding her right leg straight into the air. He spread her open and went as deep as he could, driving her crazy as her head fell back in pleasure. Dahlia could feel her release coming, but as she looked behind Po, she saw red and blue lights attached to a U.S. Coast Guard speedboat in the distance.

Right on time, she thought. In order for Dahlia to take Po's place, he would have to give it to her. She couldn't kill him and expect to step into his shoes. No, Po would have to give the streets his blessing to work with her, and she knew only one way to make that happen. Set up his downfall. Unbeknownst to Po, Dahlia had boarded the boat with a bag full of cocaine—twenty bricks, to be exact. Having given an anonymous tip to the Coast Guard, she knew that it was only a matter of time before they found the rented yacht.

"Hurry," she urged as she threw her hips at Po, trying to get hers before it was too late. Po crushed into her, and Dahlia closed her eyes and felt the rush as she reached satisfaction. She didn't even let him finish before she pushed him off of her.

"Po . . . something's wrong," she said as she sat up and nodded toward the Coast Guard. Po turned around and saw the speedboat slowing as it approached. He pulled off the condom, tossed it into the nearby garbage, and adjusted his clothing.

"Fuck is this about?" he muttered.

Dahlia's eyes widened in uncertainty as she adjusted her swimsuit.

"I'll handle it. Just let me do the talking," he assured her. She nodded, and the look of fear in her eyes could have won her an Academy Award.

Dahlia watched as Po transformed before her eyes. It was as if his high was immediately blown. He squared his shoulders, and she could see the anger pulsing through the veins that bulged in his neck as he gritted his teeth. The Coast Guard stopped several feet away. Po quickly assessed the situation. There were two men and two guns against his one. He didn't foresee the situation escalating, but he liked to know the odds he was facing, just in case. *I'm clean, nothing to worry about,* he thought.

"Can I help you, gentlemen?" he asked almost pompously.

"We have reason to believe you are carrying drugs aboard this vessel. I need to see your hands," the guardsman said sternly as he kept his hand near the gun that was holstered securely at his side.

"There are no drugs on this boat," Po scoffed. Under normal circumstances, he would have requested a warrant, but he had nothing to hide. He just wanted this encounter complete so that he could go about his business. "Be my guest." He motioned for the guardsman to come aboard. The guardsman behind the wheel maneuvered the boat so that it was aligned next to Po's and then watched as his colleague climbed aboard the luxury yacht.

The guardsman's facial expression was cold and hard as he pointed to the deck of the boat. "Sit down, both of you, on top of your hands. My partner will keep an eye on you while I search the boat," he stated harshly in a no-nonsense tone of voice. "We've got reason to believe that this boat is transporting narcotics."

"Reason to believe?" Po questioned, his irritation now apparent as he complied with the guardsman's request to sit on the deck.

"An anonymous tip," the guardsman replied. "Sit tight." He disappeared down the short staircase that led to the lower deck of the boat.

Po turned toward Dahlia and noticed the weird expression on her face. He couldn't read her, so instead of guessing, he just asked. "What's the face about, ma? There something you not telling me?"

Dahlia opened her mouth to respond, only to be interrupted by the guardsman as he emerged from the bottom deck. "Well, well, what do we have here?" In his hands, he carried a Gucci duffel bag. He revealed the contents to Po.

The invisible punch to his gut took his breath away as he saw the crystal-white kilos inside. It was so pure that it sparkled like diamonds. The fact that it was uncut was even worse. The Coast Guard would bury him under the jail just for the purity alone. Po's temper flared, and he saw red. He knew that the guardsman had not planted the drugs, because he had seen him get on the boat with nothing in hand. There was only one other person to whom the bag could belong. Po shot Dahlia a look that could kill. They were in international waters. That amount of drugs could land him in prison for the remainder of his life. This wasn't a game, and now everything was on the line.

"You're under arrest," the guardsman said.

Po calmly stood while keeping his hands in clear view. He didn't want to give them a reason to pop off. He had heard too many stories about overzealous officers to give them a reason to shoot him. Dahlia stayed seated on the deck with her head lowered. Her face revealed sorrow, but her thoughts were sinister. The boat was rented under Po's name. They would pin the drugs on him. His arrest would signify the end of his reign but the beginning of Dahlia's. With Rocko and Liberty out of the picture, Po would have no choice but to entrust his empire to her.

"You can take me in. You'll get overtime from the paper-work and a slap on the back from your boss, and then you'll go home worth the same amount that you were when you awoke this morning, or you can turn the other cheek. You found that duffel bag, but you missed the one with $150,000 down there. You and your partner can have it. It's all yours if you just do nothing. No report, no arrest, just do nothing. Just get back in your boat and ride away. That's your salary for two years in one day," Po reasoned calmly. He knew that he had the guardsman, because he was still talking. If he wasn't interested, then Po would have been in cuffs by now. He lowered his hands as the guardsmen looked back and forth between each other and him, speaking without speaking and confirming that they both were intrigued by the proposition.

"The offer is only good for the next fifteen seconds, gen-tlemen. What's it gonna be—"

Dahlia watched in utter disbelief as the guardsmen exited

the yacht with a duffel bag full of money. She had known that Po was extremely savvy, but never did she expect him to fast-talk his way out of a setup. Now she had to get her story together, because the fire that she saw in his eyes revealed his anger. As soon as the Coast Guard boat pulled away, Po aimed his wrath toward her. He turned on his heels and without warning slapped the taste from her mouth. The sting of his assault radiated through her cheek as her head whipped to the right. Her mouth fell open in an O of surprise. She was livid, shocked, and turned on all at the same time. It appeared that Po wore his crown better than she thought he did. This was a side of him that she had yet to see. It was attractive, and she realized that although he had potential, it was a shame that he was the one person who stood in the way of her takeover. He would be a casualty of the game. Her plot to get him out of her way had failed today, but she would find another way to get rid of him.

"What the fuck is twenty kilos doing on this yacht? In your bag?" he asked. "Do you know how you've put me at risk?" He radiated anger. It was so palpable that Dahlia could see his temperature rising as his skin flushed slightly.

She had to keep her own temper in check and remember the role that she was playing. "I'm sorry. We were headed to Mexico. I have a buyer down there who wants to re-up. I thought it would be smart to handle a bit of business in addition to pleasure. I didn't know we would be stopped by the fucking Coast Guard, Po," she said, her voice even but also stern. Po knew Dahlia, and the senseless slipup was completely uncharacteristic of her. She was too seasoned to make such a drastic mistake. He shook his head and squeezed the bridge of his nose to stop himself from blowing his top. Her negligence could have cost him his freedom, and she seemed too nonchalant for his taste. He gripped her shoulders roughly as he stared at her harshly, shaking her slightly as he spoke.

"What the fuck can twenty keys do for me? For us? Huh? Use your head. We don't deal drugs anymore. Leave that for the little niggas. I'm in on the diamond mines now, and you're this close to fucking that up," Po chastised as he pinched his thumb and pointer finger together. "You don't overplay your position. You come into the game when I require you to, not when you feel like it. If you can't occupy your seat, I know somebody who was doing it just fine before you came along."

Dahlia was stunned to silence at his threat as he pushed her away. The fact that he was throwing Liberty in her face meant that he wasn't truly over her. Dahlia would have to hurry and get rid of Po before fate brought Liberty and Po back together.

Po tossed the bag of cocaine to her and said, "Toss this shit overboard. We're headed back to L.A. Vacation's over." He stormed past her and headed to the captain's seat to lift the anchor. "Stupid mu'fucka," he grumbled.

Dahlia's blood boiled, but she didn't buck. She simply cut her eyes at him as he walked away, then took the bag and tossed it into the ocean.

Time to come up with plan B, she thought.

* * *

Rocko grimaced in excruciation as he sat at gunpoint in the middle of Po's foyer. His entire pant leg was soaked in his own blood from the gunshot that Zulu had delivered to his knee. It was a warning. He had let Rocko know that he had no problem with pulling triggers. There was no hesitation behind his actions. His intentions were clear, and Rocko knew that if he didn't tell Zulu what he wanted to know, then the next bullet would go through his head. Rocko squared his jaw and sat back in the chair as he gritted his teeth through the pain. He had come to Po's house to confront him about his recent actions, only to walk directly into a setup—one that wasn't even meant for him.

"I don't know where Dahlia is, but when you find the bitch, let me know," Rocko spat.

Zulu stood with his hands planted in front of his body, crossed at the wrists, as he stared seriously at Rocko. Men in all-black business suits stood behind him and were lined up on the balcony above their heads. They looked like a black regiment, strong and deadly as they loomed over him. The automatic weapons in their hands let Rocko know that they had come to kill. He didn't know exactly what Po and Dahlia had gotten themselves into, but whatever it was, things were beyond repair. If the African Mafia had come across the seas to get to L.A., they hadn't come to talk. Zulu was ready for war, and Rocko had walked right into the middle of it.

"You mean to tell me you are Po's right-hand man, and you don't know where to find him? Do not mistake me for a fool, Rocko," Zulu said. His voice was low and calm, but

Rocko could see by the look in his eyes that Zulu's murder button had been pushed. Zulu was out for blood.

"If you gone pull that trigger, you gone do it whether I tell you or not. I know the game. I know how this ends, Zulu. Go ahead. Kill me. Even when I'm gone, my name gone live on the tongues of many, and a nigga will not be able to say that I bitched up at the end. I don't know shit," Rocko stated harshly.

A flash of anger appeared in Zulu's eyes. "You're a loyal man, Rocko. Stupid but loyal," Zulu said. He raised his hand, and on cue, all of his men racked their weapons and trained them on their target.

Rocko's nostrils flared as he breathed rapidly, trying to prepare himself for death. He could hear his heart pounding in his ear. It wasn't fear that was pulsing through him. He felt a mixture of pride, regret, and anxiety as his chest swelled. He calmed himself. If he was going to die, he wasn't going out as a coward. He breathed in slowly, deeply, enjoying the feeling of his lungs expanding, because he was sure that it was the last breath he would ever take.

"Wait!"

Liberty's voice cut through the air, and instantly, all of Zulu's loyal guns were aimed her way. Her hands shot up as her eyes widened in bewilderment. She took in the entire scene. The blood made her stomach turn as she watched it pool beneath Rocko's chair.

"Leave, Liberty!" Rocko shouted.

"No, please, Liberty, join us," Zulu said. "I insist. Maybe you can give me the answers I seek."

"She has nothing to do with this, Zulu," Rocko snapped.

"I'm here now, Rocko. Don't speak for me," she replied. The tremor in her voice didn't go unnoticed.

"You're afraid," Zulu observed. "Do you know who I am?"

Liberty nodded. "I do, and I know who you're here for."

"Where are they?" Zulu asked.

Liberty looked around at the members of the African Mafia, and her heart skipped a beat. The lump that had formed in her throat stifled her response. She cleared her throat. "I might be more inclined to respond if there weren't a thousand guns pointed at me," she said.

Zulu looked at her curiously. He had heard a lot about Dahlia's long-lost cousin, the infamous Liberty, but to see her up close nearly took his breath away.

"You are quite rare," he said distractedly. "And you're from Sierra Leone?"

"I am. Born there, kidnapped, and groomed here in L.A.," she responded. "I have no problem talking pleasantries with you, Zulu, but my friend is bleeding out all over the floor. He isn't who you came for. I need you to let him go. You want someone who knows everything, then take me. Rocko is just a henchman; he can't tell you what I can. So take me."

"Loyalty runs deep here," Zulu whispered. "Weapons down." On his command, the men lowered their guns.

"Liberty, what are you doing?" Rocko asked.

"What I have to," she replied.

Zulu stepped close to Liberty, leaving no space between them. Liberty immediately recognized the smitten look in his eyes. "I may be inclined to leave here if I can take a prize back to Africa, a beautiful prize . . ." He lifted a tendril of her hair as he spoke.

"My possession is not up for negotiation. I'm not some object to be bought and sold . . ." She paused as tears came to her eyes. "Not anymore. I don't know where Po and Dahlia are."

"Then you're wasting my time," Zulu barked.

"If Po and Dahlia want to hide out forever, they have the means to do so. I can hand-deliver Dahlia to you, if you spare Po and the rest of us. You don't want Po. Dahlia is the one who turned business bad. She crossed you, not Po," Liberty said. She felt as if she were drowning as she spoke. She was clearly in over her head. Her eyes bounced around the room frantically as she looked at all of Zulu's goons. "Please."

"You beg to save the life of your friends, but you easily cross your cousin," Zulu said, intrigued.

"Blood doesn't make you family," she said. "Dahlia has betrayed me. Giving her over to you would make for such sweet revenge."

Zulu huffed unpleasantly and stared at her with such intensity that Liberty had to lower her eyes. "You have forty-eight hours to deliver Dahlia to me. Your life depends on it," Zulu conceded. He nodded toward Rocko. "Take your friend."

Liberty's legs felt like Jell-O as she rushed to Rocko's side. "Rocko," she whispered as she fell to her knees in front of him. "Oh, my God, Rocko."

"What did you do, Liberty?" he asked.

"I don't know," she replied as she placed a hand to his cheek. "I couldn't just let him kill you." She made quick work of the ropes that were binding his hands behind the chair. She could barely untie the knots, she was shaking so badly. She could feel the eyes of the men surrounding them burning into her. Finally, she freed Rocko, and he rose from the chair.

"Aghh!" he hollered out as he tried to put weight on his leg. Liberty quickly tucked herself under his arm for support, and they hobbled to the door. Liberty half expected to be shot in the back as they made their exit.

"Forty-eight hours." Zulu's voice boomed out.

She turned and nodded obediently before leaving with Rocko.

"We've got to get the fuck out of here," Rocko stated as soon as they were outside. "Aghh, fuck!" he groaned as he left a blood trail from the front door to his car.

"You're losing a lot of blood!" Liberty yelled. She looked back frantically at the house as Zulu's men began to emerge. She got Rocko secured in the passenger seat and then ran around to get in. She wasted no time in pulling away from the house.

As soon as Zulu was in her rearview, she felt her tears begin to flow. Rocko reached over and placed his hand on her shoulder.

"I need to get you to a hospital," Liberty said.

"No hospitals," Rocko protested. "There's a contact in my phone under 'Doc.' Text the number. Tell her to come to my house immediately. My address is stored in the GPS."

Rocko's pain took him into a temporary solace as he passed out beside her. Liberty's hands shook as she reached over and removed his cell from his pocket. She scrolled through his contacts and sent the urgent text. Then she took a deep breath in an attempt not to panic as she let the GPS guide her toward Rocko's home.

In all the time she had known him, she had assumed that he lived out of the trap houses that he sold from. As she drove through his well-kept neighborhood, she knew that she had been mistaken. The middle-class suburban street was beautiful, and she quickly realized that she had misjudged Rocko. She was always blind to the details when it came to him, because he was Po's friend. She never paid him too much attention, but in Po's absence, Rocko was now so clear to her. He was smart and loyal and had a rugged appeal that would make any woman lucky to call him her own. Liberty appreciated Rocko's friendship now more than ever. When Po had given up on her, Rocko had taken her side. He recognized real and could see that Dahlia was anything but.

She pulled up to the home that Rocko owned. It wasn't the estate that Po had, but it was a beautiful contemporary lot with a manicured lawn and a two-car garage. Rocko was a hustler living among doctors and lawyers. That in itself was impressive to Liberty, more so than the flashy home that she had shared with Po. Rocko knew the art of humility and modesty even when he had Gotti knots in his pocket. He wasn't trying to stunt; he was simply trying to live. Liberty pulled into the garage and then closed it so that prying eyes wouldn't see her pulling Rocko's bloody body from his car. She threw the car into park and nudged Rocko.

"Rocko, wake up. I can't get you into your house alone," she said urgently. "Rocko!" Liberty exited and ran around to his side. Opening the door, she immediately noticed that the bottom of his car was stained in red. "Please, Rocko, wake up!" she shouted. He stirred slightly, causing Liberty to breathe a sigh of relief as she lowered her head. "Come on, Rocko, just help me out. Stay awake," she pleaded. She pulled him out of the car, and all two hundred pounds of him weighed down her shoulders.

"Aghh, fuck!" Rocko howled as the pain of his injury caused him to crash back into consciousness. "Damn it, Liberty!"

"I know! I'm sorry! Just a little bit farther!" she cried.

She entered Rocko's home and guided him to the couch, where he collapsed. A mess, she was covered in blood and sweat. "Where the fuck is this doctor?" she asked, emotional.

"She's coming," Rocko said. "Come over here and sit down. You freaking out like that got a nigga thinking he dying. Come talk to me. Distract me."

Liberty shook her head as she tried to pull herself together and then sat next to Rocko. "You would think I'm the one who got shot," she cracked.

Rocko chuckled as he breathed deeply to dull the pain. For the first time, he noticed the scratches on her face, and he frowned. "What happened to you? What were you doing at Po's?"

"I was shot at, well, I think you were shot at . . . I was driving your car, and gunshots just rang out. I think Po sent someone for you," Liberty admitted. "He would never do that on his own, Rocko. Dahlia is an evil bitch. She is single-handedly turning him against everyone who loves him. I went to his house to confront them, but instead, I found you . . . like this."

Rocko's eyes went cold as he thought of his best-friend-turned-adversary. It had come to gunplay between them. He never thought he would see the day, but if Po wanted to play it that way, Rocko had no problem schooling Po at his own game. There wasn't a nigga alive who could say that he had pulled out a gun on Rocko. Rocko was a thoroughbred and always clipped his loose ends. Anyone who had tried his hand had always lost. He only wondered, if the time ever came, could he deliver the same fate to a man he had once considered to be his brother?

As if Liberty could read his thoughts, she grabbed his hand. "No, Rocko. It's Po."

"Yeah, I hear you, but Po ain't Po, if you know what I mean," he responded.

Her eyes misted, and her chin hit her chest in defeat.

Rocko lifted her chin with his finger but said nothing as he stared her in the eyes. For the first time, he saw what the hype was about. Liberty was a beauty, inside and out. Her treacherous cousin had beaten her, and the loss showed all over Liberty's face. He was always indifferent when it came to Liberty. She wasn't his concern, but now, as he stared at her, he felt sympathy.

Ding dong!

Liberty rose from the couch and rushed to the door, grateful for the interruption. The tension in the room was on full, and she exhaled in relief as she opened the door. A tall blond goddess with Caribbean-green eyes stood before her in blue scrubs, with a large bag hanging from her shoulder.

"Is he here?" was her greeting.

"Yeah, um, please come in . . . hurry." Liberty moved to the side and motioned for the goddess to come in.

She quickly went to work, using Liberty as her assistant.

"I need boiling water and as many towels as you can find," the blonde said. Liberty retrieved the items and then rushed back to Rocko. As soon as the woman touched him, Rocko growled in agony. He clenched his teeth to stop himself from waking up the entire neighborhood. Liberty stood to the side, brows furrowed as she winced, as if she could feel Rocko's pain.

"Are you a real doctor?" Liberty asked in concern.

The blonde worked diligently. "I'm a resident," she responded. "Rocko pays me very well to be available if he needs me."

Liberty watched warily and talked Rocko through his at-home surgery until the bullet was removed and the wound was sealed. Two hours later, the blonde had left, and Rocko sat with his knee wrapped and elevated as the pain pills he had taken relaxed him slightly.

"Are you OK?" Liberty asked.

"I'm a G, ma, it take a whole lot more than a bullet to the knee to take me out the game," he joked with a crooked grin. She smiled and shook her head. "The question is, are *you* OK?" he asked.

She didn't answer, because she wasn't sure.

"Time isn't on our side, ma, and quite frankly, the way I'm feeling, I might not stop Zulu from getting at Po. The nigga tried to have me hit. He almost hit you," Rocko said, his voice low and unnerving.

"He's not himself. You know he wouldn't do that. It's Dahlia, she makes him . . . different," Liberty whispered as she folded her arms in front of her chest.

"The nigga's stupid. He moving real sloppy over a bitch," Rocko said.

"In his defense, she's not an ordinary bitch," Liberty muttered. "Please, Rocko. You know Po. You know him better than I do. Just help me, help him. Help me get Dahlia."

Rocko's ego had him wanting to start a war with Po, but his heart was conflicted. They had come up together and were like brothers. Yes, Po had sent bullets his way, but Rocko was supposed to be his keeper. He felt partly responsible for allowing Dahlia to get close enough to corrupt Po.

"I can't promise you nothing, Liberty. I don't know how shit will play out when I'm face-to-face with your man. You're right. I know Po, and once he calls a play, he sticks by it, wrong or right," Rocko said.

She shook her head. "Not this time. Just talk to him first. I'll be upstairs in the guest room if you need anything."

Rocko watched her walk out of the room, and just before

she disappeared from sight, he called out to her. "Liberty . . . You still love him? After he put you out, slept with Dahlia, turned on you for your own blood. You still care about him?"

Liberty blinked slowly as she thought about his question. In her heart, she knew that she had never truly allowed herself to love Po. She had been too stuck in the past, too caught up in the memory of A'shai, even to allow Po to compete. She had pushed him away, and she accepted responsibility for the part she had played in the failing of their relationship. She nodded and finally spoke. "We both made mistakes. I just want a chance to make things right."

"You're a loyal woman, Liberty," he said as he turned from her and reached for the cognac that sat in a crystal decanter.

Liberty moved toward him and took it from his hands. "Here, let me," she said.

She poured him a glass, and her hand touched his gently as she passed it to him. He grabbed her hand, and she gasped as her heart skipped a beat. She quickly snatched her hand away.

"You never know if you're loyal until it's not easy to be," she whispered. She shook her head and forced a smile onto her face as she stood. "Now, do you have anything I can change into? This blood isn't a good look," she said, lightening the mood as she motioned to her clothing. "I can wash them tonight. I just need something to sleep in."

Rocko gave her a slight smile. It seemed awkward on his

face, because before today, she had never seen him smile. In fact, this was the most communication they had ever had. She was getting to know him for more than just his role as right-hand man, and she liked what she saw. She was learning that there was much more to the hardened hustler than what met the eye.

"Yeah, there are clothes in the closet in the guest room. One of my button-ups should do," he said as he licked his lips.

"I suppose it will," she responded. She smiled but then stopped, catching herself. *Is this flirting?* she thought guiltily as she flushed, suddenly turning red. Liberty didn't know what had changed the tides between her and Rocko, but they both knew that nothing could come of it. They were linked through Po, nothing more and nothing less.

"The laundry room is on the second floor. I don't fool around in there too much, but you can go for what you know," Rocko offered.

"Thank you," she said. "Good night, Rocko."

Her voice was like the soft melody of his favorite song. He didn't know if it was the pain medication that he was on or if he had truly been blind before, but it was as if he was suddenly seeing her for the first time. Her beauty, her appeal, her loyalty—it was all wrapped in one perfect package. She had bid him good night but hadn't moved. She stood in front of him, staring down at him as he stared up at her in silence. His bad leg was draped out as the other one was cocked in an L shape, and his arms were sprawled over the back of the couch.

"Why didn't you ever say anything to me before?" she asked.

"You belonged to Po," Rocko stated, his eyes low from the effects of the cognac.

"Is that what I'll always be? A man's possession?" Her voice was sad as her eyes misted, causing Rocko to sit up. He reached for her hand, and there it was again, that spark. Rocko released her hand instantly and leaned back on the couch. He had never been a snake, and he couldn't start now. Despite the fact that Po had tried to kill him, he still couldn't cross the line with Liberty.

"You should head to bed," Rocko insisted. "We have a long two days ahead of us."

"I can't," she whispered. "Not until I know what that is." Her voice trembled.

"What what is?" Rocko questioned.

Liberty sat on the couch next to him and grabbed his hand again, intertwining her fingers with his. Her heart sped up as he closed his fingers, sealing their grip. It felt as if a current was flowing between them as Rocko sucked in a sharp breath.

"That . . . What is that feeling between us, Rocko?" she whispered, confused by her own emotions. She looked up at him. She was lost, intrigued, and guilt-ridden all at the same time, and it showed in her gaze.

Everything about her in that moment was meant for Rocko. He could feel his body reacting to her, his loins filling with a familiar need. *Fuck is you doing?* he thought to himself. He uncurled his fingers and cleared his throat. "I need you to go upstairs, ma, before we both do something that we will later regret. This feeling . . . it is fear. We put our lives on the line together for Po today. It has us thinking unclearly. That's all it is, your fear pushing you toward a nigga that's no good for you. You belong to Po," Rocko said sternly, regaining his focus.

"He doesn't want me," Liberty replied as a tear fell down her cheek. Rocko wiped it away.

"I don't believe there is a man on this earth that doesn't want you, ma. Go to bed."

Liberty rose and retreated to the safety of the second floor.

Rocko watched her disappear up the stairs and then shook his head as he blew out a deep breath. He tilted his head back and downed the glass of dark liquor. "Po, you're a lucky mu'fucka, my nigga."

THREE

PO MANEUVERED THE YACHT INTO THE DOCK slip and immediately disembarked. He grabbed his bag and headed for his car parked at the end of the port. The trip back to L.A. had done nothing to calm his temper. He had barely avoided an arrest, and the close call had him on edge. He powered on his phone to see that he had ten missed calls, all from Li'l Mikey. A twinge of guilt shot through him as he recalled the hit he had put out on Rocko's life. He was surprised that Li'l Mikey was still living. He had half expected Rocko to lay Li'l Mikey down in the process. He listened to the first voice mail. Li'l Mikey's voice blared through the speaker.

"Big homey, you need to call me ASAP. I put that work in, but the shit went south. I've been blowing you up. Hit me."

Po quickly hung up and dialed Li'l Mikey as he slid into the passenger seat. Dahlia sat next to him, ears perked but eyes staring out of the window, pretending not to care.

"Man, where the fuck have you been? I've been blowing your phone up, homey," Li'l Mikey said as soon as he answered the phone. The urgency in his tone caused Po concern.

"Is it done?" Po asked.

"Nah, that's what I'm trying to tell you. Rocko wasn't in the whip. I swiss-cheesed that bitch only to find your girl inside," Li'l Mikey said.

Po's heart fell into his stomach, and Dahlia noticed wrinkles of tension fill his forehead.

"I will murder you, li'l nigga," Po threatened. "If one hair—"

"Nah, nah, boss man, hear me out. I love the air in my lungs, fam. When I ran up on the car to finish the job, I saw that it was her. I walked away. I left her breathing. I couldn't see through the tint—"

Po disconnected the call and sped away from the pier, headed toward his home. He had no words for Dahlia. He was too consumed with thoughts of Liberty to even care. If she had been hurt under a hit that he had green-lighted, he would have never been able to forgive himself. *Fuck was she doing in Rocko's Rover?* he thought, jealousy surfacing as he gripped the steering wheel. Dahlia had told him that Rocko and Liberty were dealing with each other intimately. Rocko had broken the G code, or so Po thought. He had picked up Liberty after Po had left her behind, which was the ultimate disrespect. Liberty had been wifey. She was more than a one-night stand. The fact that Rocko was keeping time with her burned Po to the core. It was the reason he had pushed the button on Rocko to begin with, but hearing that she was riding around the city in his best friend's whip made it all too real. *Where is she now?* Po asked himself, unable to tear his train of thought away from Liberty. He pulled onto his estate and popped the locks.

Dahlia stared at him peculiarly. "You're not coming up?" she asked, slightly irritated.

"That was my man on the phone. I've got some business to see to. I won't be long," he said.

His voice was clipped, and she sensed the coldness behind his words. She stepped out of the car, completely taken aback. She could feel Po pulling away from her. The web that she had weaved wasn't as sticky as she thought. She glared at the red taillights as she watched him pull away. Her hold on Po was slipping, and she needed things with him to be smooth if she wanted to take over his spot. Sure, she could kill him and get him out of her way for good, but that required too much dirty work. If she took the hard route, then she would have to throw her hat in the ring with a bunch of come-up kids looking to take his place once he was in the dirt. No, she needed Po's endorsement. She needed him to hand her his crown so that she could adopt his position and all of the soldiers he had riding with him, too.

She turned and headed toward the front door but halted in her tracks when she noticed the blood trail that was before her. She gasped, and her eyes darted to the house as the hairs on the back of her neck rose. Dahlia wondered if there was someone in the shadows, watching her every move. She shuddered as the nagging feeling of vulnerability haunted her. Dahlia realized that someone had been inside her home. Wishing that she was strapped, she shook her head. All of the lights were out inside. Only the pale yellow of the porch lamp illuminated the surroundings. Cautiously, she walked up the cement path and stepped onto the porch. The rapid beating of her heart thundered in her ear as her pulse quickened. She reached for the knob and then pulled her hand back as if it were hot to the touch.

Come on, Dahlia, go in the damn house, she told herself. She glanced over her shoulder and then put her key in the door and nudged it open with her shoulder. Her fingers slid against the wall to her left as she searched for the light switch.

Click.

She flipped the switch, and light illuminated the foyer. When her eyes took in the bloody mess that Zulu had left behind, she backpedaled until she was right back on the porch. She gasped in shock, and her hands flew to her mouth, covering it as her eyes grew wide. Dahlia felt like a deer in headlights as she stood, exposed, under the moonlit sky. She ran away from the house until she was in the middle of the yard. *Is there someone in there waiting for us? Who did this?* She wondered anxiously.

She picked up her phone and dialed Po. She danced around, shifting from foot to foot, as she listened to the phone ring. "Damn it, Po!" she muttered as she jammed the red button to end the call. Her eyes fell on the house. There seemed to be no movement inside. She made her way slowly to the house and crept to the kitchen, where she kept a small-caliber handgun. With the stealth of a cat, she maneuvered silently, as her mind played tricks on her.

She was just waiting for someone to jump out at her. She reached up, opening the oak cabinets, and retrieved the .45. The cold steel reassured her slightly as she went from room to room of the massive home. Dahlia searched until she was sure that she was alone. She ended up back in the same place she had begun, the bloody foyer.

"What the fuck happened here?" she asked herself aloud. Po was unreachable, and the fact that he was MIA when she needed his assistance angered her. Someone had come to the place where they laid their heads. Fortunately, they hadn't been home, but someone had been. Dahlia's mind spun as she tried to put the pieces of the unknown puzzle together. Prey. She had become the hunted, or, at the very least, Po had. She needed to know what adversary they were up against in order to survive.

BOOM! BOOM! BOOM!

Liberty raced down the stairs, heart pounding as the banging on Rocko's door sent chills down her spine. She looked at Rocko, who sat in the same spot he had been in hours before, still sipping cognac. He appeared too calm as Liberty rushed over to him.

"It's Po," he revealed as he nodded his head toward his television. He hit a button on the remote, and the TV showed split screens from the cameras that were posted around his property. Sure enough, Po was standing on his doorstep, his facial expression vexed.

Rocko reached down, grimacing slightly as pain shot through his leg. He retrieved a 9mm handgun that was tucked beneath the couch cushion. He checked the clip, clicked off the safety, and set it in his lap.

Liberty grabbed his hand. "Rocko, no," she whispered.

He pointed at the screen. "Look at his face, Liberty. He ain't here to talk," Rocko stated. "Let him in."

Liberty felt as if she was caught on a train track with two locomotives headed toward her, threatening to collide. She had to stop this clash of two street titans. They were best friends; surely they could resolve their differences without further bloodshed. She went to the door and pulled it open. His face . . . seeing the way his eyes reflected an abyss of sadness when he saw her was all it took to start her tears. Her heart ached as they stared at each other, silently yet with so much brooding in the air between them. Po had hurt her. He had crushed her spirit and snuffed out the little bit of faith that she had in him.

Liberty was the last person he expected to open the door, and he felt a tug of jealousy as he stood over her. She seemed broken as he stared into her soul, and out of habit, his hand found a place around her waist as he pulled her out onto the porch slightly, to be closer to him. He could hear her nervous breaths as she closed her eyes.

"Don't." Her voice was so fragile and low that he barely heard her, and he pressed his forehead against hers as they both closed their eyes.

"It's true," he whispered. "You're fucking with Rocko."

Liberty pulled away, shocked, but before she could deny anything, Po pushed past her, storming into Rocko's home.

"Rocko!" His bark was filled with animosity as his territorial instincts kicked in.

Liberty took off after him. "Po! No! Listen to me!" she pleaded as she pulled his arm, but he was so enraged that he snatched it away from her violently.

"Don't touch me!" he shouted as he made his way through Rocko's home. "Where is he?" Po didn't think about the fact that he had tossed Liberty away like a rag doll. He didn't care that he had disregarded her to start a relationship with her very own cousin. All he could picture in his mind was Liberty lying in Rocko's bed. He could hear her voice saying all the things that she had once said to him. He could see her doing all the things that she once did to him. The images he was conjuring up made him sick to his stomach. Seeing her standing there, shaken from a fresh sleep, wearing Rocko's shirt, hair tousled, had him ready to finish the job that Li'l Mikey had started.

"Po! It's not what you think!" Liberty shouted.

Frustrated and overwhelmed by jealousy and heartache, he lunged at her. "Arghh!" Po growled as he grabbed her arms and pushed her forcefully against the wall, pinning her to it with the weight of his body and startling Liberty. "You fucking my man?" he asked through gritted teeth. He had so much emotion in his face that she feared briefly that he would strike her. The fear was evident on her face as she cowered in his intimidating presence.

"Po!" Rocko's voice boomed as he hobbled into the hall-way on crutches.

Po looked at Liberty. His precious Liberty, who now stood before him, terrified. He looked from Rocko to Liberty, his head foggy from the lines of cocaine that he had taken on the way over. Shame washed over him as he loosened his grip on Liberty.

"Go upstairs, Liberty," Rocko said.

Liberty snatched her arms away from Po and rushed past Rocko in distress.

Po watched her retreat and immediately felt defeated.

"What are you doing, Po?" Rocko asked. "Look at you. You're in the clouds right now, my nigga. You've put so much shit up your nose you can't even think straight."

Po noticed the pistol that Rocko had tucked into his waistband. "That for me? You gone shoot me, Rock?"

"What you mean, come at you the way you came at me?" Rocko shot back. "You almost got her killed."

"Fuck was she doing in your car anyway? Huh? You never been the nigga to save a ho," Po replied. "You had no words for Liberty until I was done with her, now she sleeping in your shirts, driving your cars. You fucking after me, Rocko? That never been your style."

A light bulb went off in Rocko's head as jealousy reared its ugly head. *The nigga tried to off me because he thought I was fucking his girl,* he thought. Rocko shook his head in disgust as he realized that Po was transforming into a sloppy nigga. He was letting a woman steer his decisions and cause him to act irrationally.

"The Po I know wouldn't care . . . that is, if you was truly done with her," Rocko replied. "Look at you, bro. You're moving reckless. You're high all the fucking time. You tell Liberty to kick rocks for Dahlia? Then send shooters at me over her? Fuck is wrong with you? You know how I get down. You the only nigga who will ever get to say he shot at me and is still breathing, and that's just off GP. You won't get another freebie. I ain't never warred with a nigga of your caliber, but I ain't running, neither. We both know the outcome would be ugly. So let's get to root of the problem instead of sparking a beef that neither of us wants."

"I love her, Rock," Po admitted, pained by the thought of all he had done to disprove that fact. "I haven't loved anyone like that since Scarlett died. She has Scarlett's heart in her chest, and you're fucking her," Po stated. He was trying to stop his emotions from flowing, but his hurt was reflected in the strained tone of his voice.

Rocko had never seen his friend so vulnerable. Po never wore his heart on his sleeve under any circumstance, but today he was a man broken by a manipulative force . . . by Dahlia.

Rocko looked at him in shock. "Scarlett's heart? How do you know?"

"I paid off the doctor back in Michigan to give me the name of the patient her heart went to," Po said.

Rocko stumbled slightly, and Po sighed. He walked over to his best friend and positioned himself so that Rocko could use him as a brace. Rocko lifted his leg off the floor, grimacing as Po helped him back to the living room sofa. Rocko sat down in relief.

"You kicked Liberty out because you thought she was involved with me?" Rocko stated as he shook his head.

Po pinched the bridge of his nose. "Shit is fishy. It don't help that she answering your door in the middle of the night," he admitted.

Rocko scoffed. "I'm not fucking your girl, fam. She came to me for help after you broke her heart. That bitch Dahlia is bad news. Look at everything that has happened since she found her way into your head. Drugs? That ain't you. You got niggas coming for me. You used to trust me with your life. I'm willing to bet that Dahlia was the one who planted the seed against me."

Po was silent "I'm sorry about the leg," he stated.

"Your li'l niggas didn't do this. This is Zulu's work."

Po's back stiffened. "He's in L.A.," he stated. He knew that if Zulu had traveled all the way across the ocean to get to him, he wasn't coming in peace.

Rocko nodded in confirmation. "And he's out for blood. At first, he wanted both you and Dahlia. Liberty put her life on the line in order to save you. She promised him she would hand-deliver Dahlia to him. He gave her forty-eight hours," Rocko said.

Po took a seat and reached for the cognac, helping himself to a glass as he was silent, consumed by deep thought. He was blind to the claws that Dahlia had in his back, but he was slowly realizing that she was a snake in the grass. *Everything about her is rehearsed. Bitch is putting on an act to gain access,* he thought. He shook his head as he sipped the cognac. *I played right into her hand.*

Po thought of everything he had told Dahlia. The late nights when she had listened to him complain about Liberty. He realized that she wasn't the "hold you down" type that he had pegged her as. He had told her exactly what Liberty lacked, and Dahlia had purposefully supplied him with what was missing. It was a setup. The sex, the drugs—she had been plotting on him all along. He didn't know what she had to gain, but he did know that whatever trust he held for her was now wavering. He thought about the cocaine that had been found on the boat, and he grew enraged. *The Coast Guard was tipped off.* His gut told him Dahlia was behind all of the treachery, but his ego didn't want to believe that he had been so easily conquered. A woman had gotten into his head and caused him to switch up on everyone who had held him down. He held his head down in regret. He was ashamed of his recent actions, and his thoughts ran wild as he recalled all of the things that Dahlia had whispered in his ear. His inner voice ridiculed him for being so stupid. He was susceptible to feminine persuasion, and that made him weak. Pillow talk was the worst kind of manipulation, and Dahlia had perfected it. Guilt ate at him. He had put money on Rocko's head. He wasn't sure if that could ever be repaired. No amount of money, no words, no actions would suffice. While Po was pegging Rocko as disloyal, it was he who had broken the code.

"I fucked up," Po whispered as he sniffed to stop his running nose.

"Yeah, you did," Rocko admitted. "You built a fort around your empire and then locked yourself inside with the devil."

Po leaned forward and placed his fingertips in a steeple underneath his chin. "I owe you my life, Rock."

Rocko nodded but remained silent as he watched Po stand to his feet. "Appreciate you looking out fa' her," Po said. "I can take it from here."

* * *

Po knocked gently on the bedroom door as he pushed it open slightly. Liberty sat on the bed with her legs folded beneath her as she looked up at him. She was silent, her eyes saddened. He crossed the room and sat on the bed near her, only for her to back away until her back hit the headboard.

"Come here," he commanded.

Liberty's chest was so heavy with indecision that it felt as if she would suffocate. She had mixed feelings about the man sitting in front of her. She wanted to love him. She could feel her heart begging her mind to let it embrace Po, but she was hesitant, because she hated who he had become.

"You're on something," she commented in disdain. She hated to see him under the influence. Po was too sharp to have his mind altered by drugs. In fact, when she first met him, he had prided himself on his ability to remain clear-headed. She had seen the effects of drug use during her days on the streets, and the glossy look and his dilated pupils gave him away. It wasn't hard to see that Po was high. "What happened to you? Where is my man?" she asked. Disappointment filled her as she realized that the game was changing him. He had been a hustler before, but he had never had to operate at this level of the game. He was sucked into the abyss of the underworld, and instead of reigning over it, he was falling victim to it.

"I'm back, ma. I got lost for a minute, but I'm right here now. The coke is nothing. It's nothing, just something to take the edge off. I can kick that. It's not a concern, Liberty. I just needed something to cope," he said.

"Cope with what, Po? You talk like you lost something," she whispered harshly with a frown.

"I lost everything, ma. First Scarlett, then the baby you carried inside of you," he countered quickly. "The day you lost our baby, I lost you to the grief of it all. You never came back to me after that."

Liberty moved closer to him and cupped his handsome face in her hands. "You're forgetting the details, Po. You didn't lose me," she replied. "You chose Dahlia. You pushed me away when I needed you."

"She was a mistake," Po said. "If you forgive me, I'll spend every day of the rest of my life making you happy."

"You tried to kill Rocko," Liberty said as she shook her head in disgust. "You thought I was *fucking* Rocko."

"Forgive me," he said as he placed his hand on the back of her neck. Her pulse quickened as he planted kisses on her neck, awakening her insides as her sex clenched sweetly. She tried to pull away from him, but he refused to let her go.

"Forgive me, ma." His voice was low, sexy, and in control as he melted her with his touch, grazing the side of her cheek with the back of his hand. He touched her lips with his thumb, then kissed her chin as he made his way south.

A twinge of guilt flashed through her as she thought of Rocko. She was sure she had felt something when they kissed. This lust with Po was much different from the brief encounter she had with Rocko. *Why am I thinking about him?* Liberty asked. *That can never happen.*

She gasped as he grazed over her breasts, circling her nipples, elongating them under his expert touch.

"You missed me," Po whispered.

"Stop it, Po," she replied weakly, her defenses lowered by his touch. "You can't just show up and expect it all to go away. I don't even know who you are anymore."

Po advanced his pursuit, touching her in all the secret places that he knew turned her on.

"You hurt me." Tears clouded her eyes as she thought back to all of the changes that Po had taken her through.

He parted her thighs and slid his leg up her thigh to find that she wore no panties. "Forgive me, Liberty," he whispered into her southern lips.

Before she could respond, he sucked her swollen clit into his mouth, causing her back to arch and her legs to open farther as he nibbled on her gently.

"You love me?" he asked as he released her love button. He sucked it again, long and hard.

Did she? She wondered, confused by it all. Surely she had to feel something for this man whom she allowed to run in and out of her life. He had done everything to make her hate him, but here she was melting at his touch.

Is this love? This isn't what it felt like with A'shai, she thought.

"Yes," she whispered, for lack of a better answer. Half of her believed her words, but the other half was filled with doubt. How could she love someone who had wronged her? She was doubt-filled and worried. She had no idea where Po's true allegiance lay, but she still wanted to call him hers. Inside she knew that it wasn't even about Po. It was about winning. It was about finally beating Dahlia. Her thirst to defeat her cousin made her want to love Po, even if she was unsure about his ability to requite.

"Tell me," he demanded.

"I love you," she moaned as she moved her hips to increase the pressure on her clitoris. She said it because he wanted to hear it and she wanted to believe it. It was her leverage. Only her love would pull him away from Dahlia's hold. "Oh, my . . ."

Po ate her with intensity until she exploded, leaving her quivering with delicious spasms of pleasure. The vibrating of his cell phone brought her head out of the clouds. She looked and saw "DAHLIA" flashing on the screen. The reality of his betrayal came rushing right back to her.

"I'll handle it. You don't have to worry about Dahlia or Zulu. You stay here with Rocko until I send for you. The next time you see me, everything will be fine, ma, that's my word." He stood to leave.

"You're going back to her?" Liberty asked.

"I have to. If I don't go back tonight, I can't deliver her to Zulu tomorrow. I can't let her know that anything is different. If she gets wind that Zulu is in town, she'll run, and he will make good on his threats to kill you. I can't let that happen," Po said.

"It makes me sick to think of you with her," she whispered. "She's been behind everything, Po. Behind Trixie, behind the miscarriage—"

Po's eyes went from concerned to dark as his brow furrowed and his pupils narrowed. A flicker of anger shot through him. "What? I know her presence stressed you, ma—"

"I'm not talking about fucking stress, Po! I'm talking about sabotage! The crazy bitch poisoned me. The doctors found a drug called Plan B in my system. That is emergency contraception. I wouldn't even take aspirin while I was pregnant, Po. I didn't take the stuff I was prescribed for morning sickness. You really think I would have ingested Plan B? Dahlia must have been putting it in my food or my drinks."

Liberty pulled at the sides of her hair in frustration, because she could see doubt in Po's eyes. He thought she had lost it. Yes, she was unraveled, but she was completely sane. "I'm not crazy! Po, Dahlia is the crazy one."

Po was so livid that it felt as if his body was on fire. The look that he was giving Liberty was one of concern. *How did she deal with this alone?* he thought, feeling shame for leaving her side in the first place. "After hearing that, I'll never fuck with her. You don't have to worry about that. She was a mistake, and it's over. That's my word, ma. It's one night," he whispered. He gripped her chin to kiss her lips. "She will pay for hurting you, but you have to trust me."

"How can I?" She sighed.

She watched him walk away, feeling defeated by Dahlia once again. Warily, she watched from the bedroom window as he departed. Liberty felt that Dahlia would somehow get her claws back into Po and that he would turn on her once again.

FOUR

PO ADMIRED LIBERTY'S SILHOUETTE AS HE SAT in his car, looking up at her as she peered out of the bedroom window. He loved her; of that much he was certain, and he knew that he would sacrifice anyone to keep her safe. He put his car in drive and pulled away from the curb. He pondered the fact that Dahlia had put him at odds with everyone he cared for. Po had allowed her to make him weak. Like every great king before him, the person who had beaten him was the exact same person he had made queen. He lifted the console between his seats and removed a small baggie. The crystal-white cocaine sparkled even beneath the plastic barrier. His ego was bruised, his pride diminished, and his heart burdened. It would be so easy for him to numb the pain with one little sniff. Po opened the bag, and without hesitation, he rolled down his window and poured it out before releasing the bag itself.

Dahlia watched the time tick by as she sat waiting for

Po to come home. Cloaked in darkness, the only light was the tiny illumination from the numbers on the face of the large vintage clock. Her blood-red nails drummed on the arm of the chair, while she sat with legs crossed, in deep contemplation. Dahlia was nobody's fool. She could feel in the air when something was awry. When the headlights of Po's car announced his arrival, she didn't move. She simply waited for the car door to slam. Then she waited until she heard his key enter the lock. She was trying her hardest to control her temper. A confrontation between the two of them was the last thing that she needed. Arguing with him would make her like Liberty. It would make her a nuisance. *I need to be everything that she could not be*, Dahlia thought as she compared and contrasted her ways with those of her cousin. That's how she had gotten so close in the first place. It didn't take her long to find out the voids that Liberty left in Po's life. All it took was the art of observation, and Dahlia was Picasso when it came to that. Liberty didn't carry Po right. She didn't fuck him right. She wasn't nasty enough. She wasn't seasoned enough when it came to his business. Liberty was too much of a good girl. She was too fragile, and Po grew tired of her victim act. Dahlia slid in at the right time and gave him everything that was lacking. She had played him perfectly. Conquering him in bed had been the first step. Conquering his mind and introducing him to coke had been the second. Now she was trying to seal the deal by conquering his kingdom. She wanted to take over the streets without him knowing they had been taken, and by the time he realized that he was no longer in control, it would be too late. That was the plan, but it seemed as though something was interfering.

As Po made his way past her, she spoke. "Is everything OK, baby?"

Po clicked on a light instantly. "You scared the shit out of me. Don't do that. If I was in a different kind of mood, I could have popped you," Po said, knowing that he was a shoot-first-and-ask-questions-later kind of guy.

They stood in front of each other, awkward and silent as she tried to read him and he did the same. Po didn't understand how he had missed all the signs that she was a snake. She had deceived him with her exotic beauty, her business sense, and her sexual prowess. His dick had gotten him in trouble, and as he stared at her, it took all of his willpower not to snap her neck. She stepped closer to him, and Po looked down at her sternly, with no show of affection in his face.

"Are you mad at me, Daddy?" she asked sweetly.

Po smirked as he felt her fingernail tracing over the front of his pants. "Did you do something that I should be mad about?" he replied.

Dahlia smiled and scoffed. "I'm always a bad girl, Po," she said sweetly as she massaged his dick. She could feel it hardening beneath her touch. She was like a snake charmer. His dick was under her control. "I can think of a few punishments that I deserve."

Po's reaction to her was purely physical, but his mental self was no longer blind to her acts of betrayal. He grabbed her by her face with one hand, squeezing her cheeks together as he glared at her.

His aggression slightly startled Dahlia, but she never stopped stroking him. "Punish me, Po," she whispered.

Po pushed her back against the wall with so much force that the pictures hanging on it fell to the floor. Dahlia winced slightly as she simultaneously ripped open his shirt. She went in for a kiss, but Po turned his head and gripped her shoulder to push her down to her knees. Dahlia was eager to please. Sex had always been her way to weaken his defenses, and he clearly had his guard way up. She needed him to lower it, and an orgasm was just the way to do it . . . or so she thought. She unzipped his linen pants and took all of him into her mouth. Po fisted his hands through her hair and pumped her with ferocity, causing her to gag slightly from his roughness. He pulled her hair so tightly that it hurt, but she didn't complain or stop. Po thrust into her without regard for her comfort, making her head bob every time he stroked. He held her in place so that she couldn't run from him. Her only option was to take all of him in until he finally exploded. Dahlia tried to pull away, but he didn't loosen his grip until he was ready to let her go. When he was finished, he zipped his pants and walked out of the room without words, leaving her stunned, with tears of fury glistening in her eyes.

"You can put the call in to Zulu. I just got word from Po."

Rocko's voice startled Liberty, bringing her back to the present, where she found herself staring blankly into the bathroom mirror.

"You all right?" Rocko asked as he noticed her dismal expression. She stood, disheveled inside and out. Yesterday's clothes sat folded on the sink, still showing traces of the blood that had destroyed them. No washing machine could get those stains out. He walked into the bathroom and stood behind her. He smiled. "Looks like I owe you a new outfit."

"Yves Saint Laurent," she muttered with a chuckle as she lowered her head and gripped the sides of the porcelain sink. She sighed as she tried to release the tension from her body.

"Hey, hey, what's wrong? You know everything is going to go smoothly today. Po's back on our team. Dahlia will get what's coming to her. Everything's good," Rocko said, still looking at her through the mirror.

She lifted her head. "You know what I was thinking about before you walked in?" she asked rhetorically. "I was thinking of Dahlia, back in Sierra Leone. I used to love her when we were kids, when all along I think she's always secretly hated me. She has done the unforgivable, and still I'm sick over the fact that I'm about to hand her over to Zulu. He's gonna kill her. She's my blood, Rocko. No matter how I justify it, it doesn't feel right."

Rocko could see her torment. Her beautiful face was sad, uncertain, and plagued with burden. Her kind heart was one of the many things that made her so different from all of the females he knew. She was compassionate—in this case, to a fault. "She started this, Liberty, and whether you give her up or not, Zulu will eventually find her. It's her or you. What you have to ask yourself is this: Would Dahlia hesitate if the shoe was on the other foot?"

Rocko was standing so close to her that she felt his breath on her neck. She could smell the scent of his Armani cologne. For some reason, their blossoming friendship was so comfortable to her. It was as if she had known Rocko forever. She didn't know if Po would come through for her today, but she felt a sense of security knowing that at least Rocko would be there no matter what. How quickly things had changed. She looked up at his reflection in the mirror. She could see his concern for her.

"Rocko, about last night . . ."

"Nothing needs to be said, ma. You were vulnerable. I was standing where Po should have been. It was easy to get confused," Rocko said. "It's dust under the rug."

Liberty smiled and turned toward him. "You're a great guy, Rocko. You deserve a nice girl, someone to take care of you. I hope you find that," she whispered sincerely.

Rocko smirked and bit his lower lip. He shook his head as he grinned. He had never smiled so much in his life than when he was in Liberty's presence. The hard goon had found his kryptonite, and inside he was slightly relieved that she could never be his girl. She would be a weakness if she belonged to him. Liberty had a way of softening even the most seasoned gangster, and she was working her magic on Rocko without even trying. "Not gonna happen."

"What? Why not?" she asked.

Rocko leaned in and whispered in her ear, "Because all of the good girls are taken."

Rocko turned to leave, and Liberty suddenly felt desperate for him to stay. Their encounter had ended too quickly. Their conversation flowed so easily. Everything about the two of them felt natural. *Why is he walking away from me?* she thought in a slight panic. The familiar spark that she felt in Rocko's presence was never felt with Po, but she knew what it was, because she had only felt it with one other person in her life, A'shai. Rocko gave her butterflies.

"Rocko!" she belted, his name coming out with urgency and louder than she had intended. He turned around, and on a whim, she rushed him, pressing her lips against his as her body melted into him. The fullness of his lips . . . the way his strong arms wrapped around her slim waist, pulling her protectively close . . . the electricity she felt as they kissed passionately. It was all so raw and unfiltered that it just felt . . . good. He pulled away from her, but she wouldn't let go. Rocko gave her that A'shai feeling. How could she let go? She rubbed the sides of his face as he rested his forehead against hers, eyes closed in anguish.

"Liberty . . ."

"I know it's wrong," she whispered hurriedly. Their internal struggle was clear. What was the purpose of all of this if she didn't want to be with Po?

"You're not mine, Liberty," he whispered. He wiped her lips with his thumb and index finger gently, but he never removed his forehead from hers. "We can't do this."

"Then why are we both still standing here?" she replied.

Liberty's sudden interest in him had Rocko's head spinning. She was intoxicating, and standing so close to her made it hard for him to gather his thoughts. His body and his heart were pulling him toward her, but his mind knew that this was a direct violation of the G code. He was going against everything that he stood for. Even if Po didn't deserve Liberty, it wasn't Rocko's job to say so. *Walk away,* he told himself, but her delicate hands were rubbing his face so lovingly that she had him in a trance. As he looked into Liberty's eyes, he was certain that he had just discovered the eighth wonder of the world. Rocko had never loved any woman, not even his own mother. He was a motherless child, a lost soul, and the feelings that Liberty was stirring up within him were foreign. The weight of his own heart scared him. It was as if in twenty-four short hours, Liberty had melted the ice around a heart that had been frozen for twenty-seven years.

"We could run," Liberty whispered. "Run away from L.A. . . ." She paused nervously as she looked at him. So much fear rested in her gaze. "We could run . . . together." She said the last part so low that he almost missed it.

"I don't run," he whispered. "And this is fear, ma. That's all it is. You're afraid of Zulu, of Dahlia, and now you're afraid that Po might hurt you again. The only person you don't fear is me. I'm comfort, that's all." Rocko removed her hands from his face. Even he didn't believe his own words. The hold that Liberty had on him was too strong to be something as superficial as fear, but he would never call it what it really was. It was too inappropriate to speak into existence. He couldn't care for Po's girl. For the first time, Rocko understood why Po had gone back to save Liberty from Samad. There was just something about her. Once she put her spell on you, it was hard to break.

"You belong to Po," Rocko said. He saw her face fall in disappointment and felt a stab on the left side of his chest. "Make the call to Zulu, and do me a favor, Liberty. Stay here while Po and I handle it. I don't want anything to happen to you. I would never forgive myself."

"You can't say no to me and then make me your responsibility. Don't do that. Don't confuse things. If you want it to be the way that it was, then go back to being invisible, but don't act like you care and expect me not to do anything about it. I belong to Po," she reminded him. "So I'm coming."

Rocko sighed. He wasn't up for an argument. He didn't have time for the back-and-forth. Liberty was protesting to be difficult when it was in the best interest for everyone if she stayed behind. "Put in the call, then get dressed," he said. He stepped out. He heard the shower begin to run, and he waited a few minutes outside the door. When he was sure that she was in the shower, he opened the door and quietly snatched her phone. He looked at the screen and saw the text from Zulu that disclosed the meeting place. Rocko grabbed his keys and left, leaving Liberty behind.

FIVE

THE SILENCE THAT FILLED THE ROOM WAS deafening as Dahlia sat at the vanity applying black lipstick to her full lips. She eyed Po through the mirror as he dressed behind her. He meticulously loaded two pistols and checked the clips before placing them carefully in his shoulder holster. The stern and focused look on his face caused her great concern.

"You act as if you're preparing for a shootout," she commented without turning to look at him as she continued to apply her makeup.

Po came up behind her and placed his hands on her shoulders. "I'd rather be caught with them than without," he commented. "Hurry. I need you to ride with me today. I have a meeting, and I need you to be my second set of eyes. That was Rocko's job, but I can't trust him, right?" Po asked.

Dahlia looked up at him. "If Rocko would sleep with

Liberty, what other lines would he cross?" she asked rhetorically.

Po nodded. "You're right. Then it's me and you. I just hope I can trust you."

"Have I given you reason not to?" she replied.

BUZZZ.

The sound of Po's vibrating phone saved him from a reply. He checked it.

Po smirked and put his phone away, then gave her shoulders a squeeze before he walked out of the room. Just before he disappeared from sight, he said, "Be ready to leave within the hour."

Liberty exited the shower and wrapped a towel around her body. She went to reach for her clothes and frowned when she noticed that her phone was no longer sitting next to them. She lifted the clothes and searched the floor around her, but her efforts were useless. In her heart, she knew that Rocko had taken it. She shot out of the bathroom.

"Rocko!" she shouted as she stormed to his room. It was empty. "Damn it, Rocko!" She made her way to the first floor. "Rocko!"

She realized that he had left her there when she went into the garage only to find that his car was gone. "What the fuck!" she exclaimed. She ran to Rocko's house phone and snatched it off of the base. She quickly dialed her own cell number. When it went to voice mail, she felt a slight panic settle into her bones. "Grrr!" she screamed in frustration. She rushed back up the stairs to dress. Liberty could not let the meeting with Zulu go down without her. She didn't care if it wasn't safe, she just wanted to be there to see Dahlia's face the moment she realized she had been betrayed. If Dahlia didn't know that Liberty was behind the setup, then it defeated the purpose. Dahlia had to know that this time, she had lost to the cousin she had underestimated. She quickly put on her bloodstained clothes and rushed down the steps. She swung open the door and ran face-first into the devil.

"Where are we going?" Dahlia asked, looking out the window as Po silently brooded while he drove through the city streets, one hand gripping the steering wheel.

He didn't answer, but his vibe was throwing her off. She had never been one to ignore her intuition, and it was throwing up red flags. Ever since they had stepped foot off the yacht, his demeanor had changed. The way that he had handled her the night before when they had sex was uncharacteristic of Po, who was usually such a gentle lover, yet he had fucked her harshly, disrespecting her in the process. Dahlia was no fool. She felt that Po had abandoned her team and wherever he was driving her wasn't for her own good. Dahlia reached into her bag, knowing that once she made her next move, the jig would be up. She palmed the small pistol inside her purse and looked over at Po. The icy expression on his face gave him away, and without further thought, Dahlia drew her gun and dug it into Po's side.

"Pull the car over, Po," she said calmly.

"What the fuck are you doing?" he shouted as he glanced at the gun in alarm.

"I won't repeat myself. You have ten seconds before I put holes in your stomach," Dahlia threatened.

Po lifted his fingers off the steering wheel while keeping his palm in place to guide the car. "A'ight, a'ight," he said as he pulled over to the side of the road.

"Give me your fucking phone," Dahlia said through gritted teeth as she jabbed him deep in the side with the gun. "Hurry up!"

Po clenched his jaw and reached to his waist, but Dahlia stopped him. "Don't play with me, Po. I will blow your head off. Put your hands on the steering wheel." She reached over and snatched both pistols out of his shoulder holster. Po exhaled sharply, and his nostrils flared in anger.

She then pulled his phone from his jacket pocket and slid the unlock button across the screen. It opened to the text message that Rocko had sent. Her brow furrowed.

"Rocko, huh?" Dahlia said. "You were driving me into a setup. And if you're back in cahoots with Rocko, that means you've made up with Liberty." She laughed cockily. "Was my dear cousin plotting revenge? You should know better than to think that simple ass Liberty can beat me."

"I don't fuck with Liberty. I'm meeting Rocko because he got a diamond buyer with him. I wanted you with me to be my backup," Po lied, coming up with a cover story quickly. "Fuck a bitch, Dahlia, you know the game. It's about the money. Rocko is good money."

Before Dahlia could respond, her own phone rang. An

unfamiliar number popped up on her screen. A select few people knew her number, and she immediately answered. She moved the gun from Po's gut to his head to keep him in check as she said, "Who is this?"

"Hello, cousin."

"Liberty, Liberty, you are full of surprises." She chuckled. "What did you do to get Po back under your thumb? I told you what would happen if you got in my way."

BOOM!

Dahlia barely moved the gun as she fired it next to Po's head.

"Agghh!" The blast was so loud that it deafened Po. His ears began to ring, and the world around him went temporarily mute.

"Dahlia! If you hurt him!" Liberty screamed.

"What? Liberty? Huh? What will you do? You're pathetic. You're weak! You always have been!" Dahlia hollered into the phone.

"Yeah, well, not this time," Liberty said. "This time, you fucked up. I have the security tapes from the house the day you killed Trixie. And unless you bring your black ass to me with Po unharmed, I'm sending them to the police." Liberty was bluffing. There were no tapes. There was no evidence, but Dahlia didn't know that. Liberty knew that Dahlia wouldn't leave such a crucial string untied. It was the perfect bait to lure her in.

"You wouldn't dare," Dahlia scoffed.

"I've lost everything, bitch," Liberty said. "Try me."

Dahlia looked over at Po. "Get out of the car!" she ordered.

"Dahlia . . ."

"Shut the fuck up and get out of the car!" she bellowed. Dahlia nudged Po's head with the gun, forcing him to open the door as she simultaneously held the phone in place with her other hand.

"I want him here unharmed, Dahlia," Liberty said.

Dahlia got out of the car and opened the trunk. "Get in."

Po gave her the coldest look as he reluctantly climbed inside. "I'm gonna kill you."

Dahlia slammed the trunk closed. "Yeah, yeah, shut the fuck up."

She looked around to make sure that no one was watching, and then she rushed to the driver's seat.

"How do I know you haven't made copies?" she asked, worried.

"Because I said I didn't," Liberty said.

"I want that fucking tape, you bitch!" she yelled into the phone.

"Of course you do. You have fifteen minutes to get here," Liberty replied. She gave Dahlia the address and then disconnected the call. She turned toward Zulu with shaky hands and handed him the phone. "She's on her way."

"Fuck is this nigga at?" Rocko said aloud as he looked around. The shipyard was empty. There wasn't a car in sight, and Rocko's patience was growing thin. All of his calls were being sent to Po's voice mail, and even when he dialed his own home, no one answered. "Something's off," he whispered. He grimaced as he adjusted in his seat, sending pains pulsing up and down his leg. He was an injured soldier, no doubt, but his two 9mms evened him out. He was fearless in the face of danger and couldn't let Po walk into a meeting with Zulu unprotected. Even through their differences, he still felt an obligation to hold him down, bum leg and all. Rocko was growing restless. He started the car as he tried to decide whether to stay or leave. He had the overwhelming desire to check on Liberty. Now that things were so quiet at the meeting place, he had a feeling that things her way weren't so safe. Somehow he felt it in his bones that Liberty was in trouble, and with Po unavailable, he concluded that Dahlia had once again gained the upper hand.

Dahlia pulled up to the house and pulled Po out of the trunk. She was so full of fury that her heart thundered rapidly. "I'm going to kill your pretty little Liberty. She's going to hand over this fucking tape, and then I'm going to put a bullet between her eyes," Dahlia said.

Po didn't know why Liberty had lured Dahlia to Rocko's home, but he heard Dahlia's threats loud and clear. Armed and full of hatred, Dahlia wasn't speaking recklessly. She meant every word that fell from her mouth. Suddenly, Po spun on Dahlia and swiftly hit her with a sharp left. The blow sent Dahlia and the gun flying to the ground. Po quickly retrieved the gun and then yoked Dahlia up as if she weighed nothing. He looked around, not wanting to create a stir in the affluent neighborhood, and pushed Dahlia toward the house. "Getcha ass inside," he growled. The charade was up. There was nothing but hostility between the two as she shuffled into the house, rolling her eyes.

"You're not going to shoot me, Po," she began as she stepped up onto the porch. The front door swung open, and Dahlia stared into the face of the devil himself.

"No, he isn't," Zulu stated. "I am."

Dahlia turned to run, but Po was behind her, blocking her path.

"Please," she whispered. All of a sudden, Dahlia turned into a ball of humility as her eyes widened and tears accumulated.

"Bring her inside," Zulu commanded.

Zulu's men surrounded him like a pack. Zulu traveled nowhere without the African Mafia. Two of his soldiers grabbed Dahlia.

"No! No!" she screamed, but she was quickly silenced as a salty hand covered her mouth. She bucked and contorted her body as she struggled against the men. Her efforts proved futile as they delivered her to Zulu's feet, dumping her into a mess before him. Liberty stood when she saw Dahlia, and they locked eyes.

"Liberty . . ." Dahlia whispered through snot and tears.

Liberty sneered at Dahlia, unable to hold in her disgust. "I hope you die slow, you heartless bitch." She slapped Dahlia with all of her might.

"Let's go," Po said. He looked at Zulu, who stared at him in contempt.

"You're done in this business," Zulu said.

Po nodded his head and then looked at Liberty before

staring Zulu in the eyes sternly. "All of our business is dead."

Zulu glanced at Liberty briefly. The dictator in him wanted to murk her just because he knew that she was the weak spot in Po's life. His affection for Liberty made him vulnerable. However, Zulu was a man of principles, and he had already promised peace upon Dahlia's delivery. "You have my word," he confirmed.

Po placed his hand on the small of Liberty's back and guided her out of the house. As soon as they stepped onto the pavement, Rocko came racing up the driveway. Po ushered Liberty to Rocko's car.

"What the fuck?" Rocko shouted.

"Just drive away from this mu'fucka. I'll explain on the way."

Rocko pulled away from his home and asked, "On the way where?"

Liberty sat back against the backseat and leaned her head back, her soul weary. Rocko stared at her through the rearview mirror. Their eyes met.

"Just take me away from here, Rocko, away from L.A. . . . Take me back to Detroit."

SIX

BLOOD. PAIN. REGRET.

Dahlia cringed on the floor as the impact from Zulu's blow caused her to collapse onto her hands.

"You dirty, dirty bitch," Zulu spat. His men surrounded them, all armed, as they watched Zulu prepare to take Dahlia's life.

"Please, Zulu," Dahlia whispered as she sat back up, coming onto her knees as she wiped the blood from her busted lip.

Zulu grunted and extended his palm to the man who stood at his side. "Salim, the machete," he said.

Salim had been Zulu's counsel for the past twenty years. He stood loyally beside Zulu. His presence seemed out of place among the men suited in expensive threads. Salim wore a beautiful dashiki, reflecting his African culture. Prestige and regality emanated from him. He stared directly at Dahlia with no sympathy. He had been through this before with

Zulu. He had played assistant to the grim reaper countless times. Dahlia had crossed one of the most powerful men in all of Africa. Now her time to pay had come.

Salim unfolded Zulu's murder weapon of choice and handed it to him. Dahlia lowered her head as a stifled cry escaped her lips. She trembled, and for the first time since her childhood, she felt fear. It was true what people said in the face of danger. Her life flashed quickly before her eyes, and she wondered when she had become so cold. Was it the day her father died? Was it the day her village was raided? Or was it much later? Dahlia's judgment day had arrived, and she was certain that she had earned a warm bed in hell.

The jagged edges of the metal proved that the machete had been used many times before. It had cut off more heads and limbs than Zulu could count.

Feelings of regret, of embarrassment, of seething rage, and of pure fear caused confusion within her. She was so terrified that she couldn't think.

"Please, Zulu . . . please," she begged as she gripped the carpet, bracing herself for the brutal way in which she was about to die. She hoped that the blade was sharp enough to kill her in one swing. She didn't want to be hacked to pieces. She didn't want to feel every blow. That was a fate that reminded her of the war back in Sierra Leone. It was a fate that no one should have to endure.

"Now you beg," Zulu said as he admired his machete.

"You can't do this," Dahlia whispered, her voice shaking and frantic.

Zulu lifted the machete.

"Please!"

He swung, and his eyes widened as he put force behind his arms.

"I'm your daughter!"

Zulu stopped just before he got to her neck, still nicking her slightly, causing a tiny trickle of blood to flow. "What?" He gasped.

"I'm your daughter!" Dahlia cried. She never lifted her head to him. Her limbs were so unstable that she shook violently. "I'm your daughter. Please, don't kill me."

Zulu thought of all of the sexual things that they had done together. Dahlia had seduced him. She had taped their encounter. She knew his secret fetishes.

"This can't be," he whispered, unsure, taken aback by her outlandish revelation.

"It's true," she answered, her voice quivering. "My mother was a whore in the red-light district in Sierra Leone. You were her most faithful client." She spoke so fast that he could barely process her words. "Her name was Myeea."

Zulu dropped the machete at his feet in shock. He hadn't heard that name in twenty years, but it still knocked the air from his lungs. "No . . ."

"It is true, Zulu. I swear to you," she urged, finally lifting her head.

Zulu knelt before Dahlia and grabbed her shoulders, forcing her to look up at him. He frowned as he examined her, studying the features of her face. He couldn't see himself. He was trying to confirm her claims any way that he could. "If you are lying . . ."

"I'm not! Zulu, I'm not. I know that I'm fucked up, but I haven't had anyone, not a mother or a father, since the rebels raided my village when I was a little girl. I'm fucked up, but I am your daughter. My mother told me. She pointed you out to me one day as you were riding through our village. I never forgot your face," she whispered.

Zulu lifted her to her feet and said, "Wait outside. Leave us."

His men began to exit the home without question.

Once they were alone, Zulu said, "Tell me. Tell me why you think I'm your father. Share with me the story your mother told you."

Dahlia listened to the sounds of passion that flowed from the room as she peeked through the slight crack in the closet door. Her mother's smooth dark skin was a stark contrast to the white body that humped wildly on top of her. Dahlia scrunched her face as her eyes swept over the hairy man who stood behind her mother, with his pants pulled all the way down to his ankles, red pimples covering his bare back. Her eyes darted to the nightstand where his wallet lay and then back to the scene going down on the bed. Nightstand . . . bed. Nightstand . . . bed. She crept out of the closet silently. The man was too involved in her mother, Myeea, to notice Dahlia as she lifted the leather wallet. She quickly opened it and saw the billfold full of money. She pulled out three bills and then put the wallet back on the nightstand before slinking back into the closet. She left the closet cracked so that she could see what was going on inside the room. The panting and fast pace of the sexual scene before her made her stomach turn. She hated witnessing her mother at work. It made her young heart sad to see her share her body with strange men all for the sake of a dollar. Finally, she heard the familiar grunts that meant the end was near.

The sweaty man peeled himself off of Myeea, who grabbed her satin robe and lit a cigarette. She leaned back against the headboard and said, "Leave the money on the table on your way out."

"The pussy was loose," the man said. "I should get a discount."

"Fuck your discount, white boy. Put your money on the table," Myeea replied.

The man grumbled as he buttoned up his shirt, snatched his wallet off the nightstand, and, without paying attention, pulled out two bills. He left the motel without even knowing that he had been hustled.

Myeea put the chain on the door behind him and then called out, "Coast is clear, baby, come on out!" She rushed to the bathroom and left the door wide open as she hoisted her leg up on the sink. "You did good, baby," she said to Dahlia.

Dahlia peered into the bathroom and watched as her mother wet the washcloth. She wiped herself clean, unashamed as she spoke to her daughter as if the routine was normal. She dressed and then grabbed her small overnight bag before leaving, clasping Dahlia's hand as they walked out onto the busy street.

Dahlia was quiet as they maneuvered their way through the traffic to hail a cab.

"You hungry, baby? You did so good that we can eat in a real restaurant tonight. We can stay in the city, have dinner, before I head back to work?" Myeea asked.

Dahlia nodded and gave her mother a half, dismal smile.

"What's wrong, baby?" Myeea asked as she stopped walking in the middle of the sidewalk and knelt down so that she was face-to-face with her child.

"I don't like watching you with your men. I miss Daddy. You never had to do this when he was alive," Dahlia said.

Myeea stood and grabbed Dahlia's hand, then hailed a cab. "Come on, baby, let me show you something." They climbed into the back of the taxi, and Myeea told the driver their destination.

"We're going to District Seven," she said.

"I don't go to District Seven," the driver said.

Myeea threw a few extra dollars into the front seat. "This cab has wheels, so it goes wherever you're paid to go. District Seven!" she shouted aggressively. She turned her attention back to Dahlia as she pulled a cigarette from her bra and lit it. Her sex-ruffled hair blew lightly in the wind as Dahlia looked up at her.

"I know you miss your daddy, Dahlia. I know times were easier when he was around, but this is all I know. I was doing this before your daddy came along and saved me. Now that he's gone, it's the only way I know to survive. You do what you know, what you're good at. I'm good at sex," Myeea said as she inhaled the nicotine into her lungs. "I have something to tell you, Dahlia, but when I do, I want you to know that this doesn't change how much Ramil loved you."

Dahlia's eyes grew wide in nervous curiosity as Myeea spoke of her father. Somehow she knew that whatever revelation her mother was about to make would change her life forever.

"He wasn't your real daddy. Your blood father was not the man you grew up with," Myeea said. "I met your real daddy doing this. He was one of the men you hate so much. Never look down on me for what I do or the men who come to me. Some of them are just lonely. You were born from it, and if it wasn't for these men, I wouldn't be able to feed you now."

The realization hit Dahlia like a ton of bricks as memories of the man she had grown up with flooded her brain. Tears misted in her eyes.

"Oh, no need to cry, dear daughter. Your blood is strong. Your daddy was much more powerful then Ramil," Myeea said. "Do you want to see him?"

A part of Dahlia wanted to scream no, but how could she not wonder who this man was? She nodded, and Myeea reached over to grab her hand. She bossily directed the cabbie until he was a block away from a known drug area.

The driver nervously checked his surroundings using his rearview mirror. "I will drop you off here, lady. I do not wait. You will have to find your own way back." His voice shook slightly from paranoia.

"We won't be getting out," Myeea replied. She pointed to a crowd of men standing outside a raggedy multihome building. "You see that man, the one with the huge diamond hanging from his neck? He's wearing the silk shirt and the black sunglasses?"

Dahlia craned her neck to see.

"That is Zulu. He is your father," Myeea explained.

Dahlia took in his appearance. He seemed strong, handsome, and in charge. All of the other men on the block catered to him as he stood among them, the obvious leader. "Is he rich?"

"He is." Myeea chuckled.

"Then why are we poor?" Dahlia asked with the beautiful naivety that only comes with childhood.

Myeea gripped Dahlia's chin and replied, "Because I didn't charge him enough to make me go away. Never let a man outwit you, Dahlia. You be the one doing the manipulating. Your mama learned that the hard way. There was no way that he would claim a whore as a wife and the mother to his child. I knew this, so I never told him. I met Ramil. He helped me. He moved me out of the city and into the villages in the countryside. We fell in love, and he vowed to be a better father to you than Zulu could ever have been."

Dahlia's eyes never left Zulu as she listened. "That's my father."

"Yeah, that's the son of a bitch . . ."

Dahlia could see Zulu's faith in her as she told her tale. The more she spoke, the more he believed. Floods of relief washed over her as she realized that he would spare her.

"I have a daughter. You are my child," he whispered as a perplexed look crossed his face. So many things made this wrong. He remembered frequenting the red-light district and having his pick of the litter among the girls. He had been reckless back then, a young, flashy, stupid kid who had left his seed inside almost every woman he had ever seduced. He knew that Dahlia could indeed be his. Distracted and confused, Zulu felt his focus had shifted. Dahlia had thrown him off of his square. He couldn't possibly think straight. He completely forgot that just moments before, he had almost made her a victim to his infamous blade.

As Zulu ran through his memories, recalling the time he had spent with the prostitute, Dahlia's mind was only on her own survival. Zulu turned away from her, and as soon as he did, Dahlia bent down and picked up the machete. Zulu was so off guard that he never saw it coming. He spun toward her, and Dahlia pushed the blade through his abdomen with all of her might and then sliced across before bringing the blade upward.

Zulu gasped in shock, gripping her hand as it held the machete. "But you're my child."

Dahlia smirked as Zulu fell to his knees and blood poured from his body. Dahlia still hadn't released the blade. "No, Zulu. I'm not your fucking daughter. I'm just a hell of a storyteller," she said sinisterly. She knew that Zulu had frequently lain with her prostitute mother. Her mother had often bragged of her important clientele, especially Zulu. Dahlia had played on that knowledge to concoct a tale that would throw Zulu off guard. Everything out of her mouth had been a creation of her imagination. She was willing to pull out the most extreme lies to cheat death, and Zulu had fed right into them. It was known that he had always desired to experience parenthood. His wife back in Africa had been unable to carry children. Her many miscarriages were public knowledge, as was his thirst to be a father. Dahlia had manipulated that fact, and the result had been deadly.

She let go of the machete and watched Zulu gurgle on his own blood. She felt no remorse as she watched him take his final breath. She stepped over Zulu's body, and her head spun. His goons were right outside, there was nowhere to run, and they were like dogs: if she showed fear, they would attack. *I have to face them*, she thought. *I have done what none of them would ever have the balls to do. They better fear me. You can show no intimidation, Dahlia. Don't fear them*. She coached herself silently as she began to step toward the front door. When she reached for the knob, she noticed that she was shaking. She closed her hand and struggled to breathe. It felt as if all the air was being sucked out of the room.

"You can do this," she whispered, and shut her eyes tightly. Liberty's and Po's smug grins entered her mind as she thought of how they had conspired to set her up. A flame started instantly in her heart as she thought of them, together, two against one. Liberty had finally won a round against Dahlia. The fact that her meager and weak adversary had gained the upper hand burned her inside. *When I find her, I am going to make her wish she had taken my advice and stayed away. She should have never fucked with me*, Dahlia thought.

She snatched open the door and walked out into the yard.

Zulu's men expected their leader to emerge, but when they saw Dahlia's face, they immediately aimed their weapons.

Salim stepped forward when he noticed the blood on her hands. He motioned for the men to wait as he approached her. "Where is—"

"Zulu is dead," she said to him as the other goons looked on. "These men can pull the triggers and avenge his death, or you can respect me for doing what you could not. How long did you serve as counsel to Zulu? Fifteen years? Twenty?"

Salim squared his shoulders proudly. "Twenty years," he stated.

"And you have not expanded into your own yet? You put in all that work, and for what? No one wants to be second in command forever." Dahlia spoke condescendingly, and her tone was hushed yet urgent. "You can join me, get these men to be my muscle now, tell them to follow me as I build a new empire!"

"You want to enter the diamond game?" Salim asked.

"I want to take over the game, every game, drugs, diamonds . . ."

All eyes were on her, and she no longer felt intimidated. If they wanted to kill her, she would be dead already. She had their attention. All she had to do was keep it.

"What Zulu was paying you, I will double. You can't go back to Sierra Leone with no leadership," she said.

"You are an ambitious girl," Salim stated. "But these men will not follow you without the endorsement of the five families. You cannot pick the game. This game chooses you, and until your involvement is approved by the families, these men will be loyal to the highest bidder. Their loyalty to Zulu wasn't about money; it was about affiliation. He was backed by the five families for a long time."

"Then we go to Sierra Leone to meet with the families," Dahlia said, determined.

"That isn't your only problem, Ms. Dahlia," Salim said.

"What else could be bigger?" she asked.

"Ali Akban," Salim said.

Dahlia gasped. "Ali Akban is dead."

"I assure you, he breathes just as you and I do. I will explain in the car. Please, this way," Salim said. He extended his hand and then announced, "Dahlia is Zulu's replacement. We will travel to Sierra Leone to have it solidified by the five families."

He instructed three of the men to stay behind and clean up the scene. Zulu had reigned for more than two decades, and Salim refused to leave his body to rot. It would be transported back to Africa so that a proper burial could be arranged. He opened the door for Dahlia, and she climbed into the backseat of the black Tahoe. Salim walked around the car and entered from the other side, then instructed the driver to pull away.

He was silent, mysterious, as he looked out his window at the passing blur of L.A.'s streets. Dahlia watched him, unsure, and she was filled with relief when he finally began to speak.

"Ali Akban was Zulu's right-hand man back in the day. When they first started out, they hustled together, starting with guns, drugs, the small stuff. Their small hustle grew to something beautiful after only five years, but like all great partnerships between men, a woman tore them apart. Ali fell in love with Zulu's wife, Harrah. When she became pregnant, he discovered the affair. Ali could not hide his affections for her. He was risky, and in public, he favored her very much. Even I could see the love he had for Harrah just from the way he stared at her. Zulu was hard on Harrah. He chastised her often in public, humiliated her in front of his soldiers. One day, Ali had seen enough and came to her defense. It was that gesture that gave him away. That very same night, Zulu beat Harrah so badly that she lost the child and would never be able to carry a baby to full term again. He sent goons to kill Ali. They burned down his house, thinking that he would be burned alive inside. Harrah, however, had warned Ali that Zulu was coming. She saved his life that day. Ali fled Sierra Leone and hasn't been heard from since. It has been eighteen years since anyone has laid eyes on him. But Zulu's death will ring out across the entire continent. It will travel across the tongues of the people like pollen on flowers, and when Ali hears that Zulu is dead, he will come. He will want to fill his spot, the same spot that you seek. If he makes it in front of the five families before you do, they will endorse him. They are familiar with him. You are a risk. A stranger. And you break all of the rules. The heads of the families are elders, Ms. Dahlia. You are a woman. You contradict everything that they think a woman should be."

Dahlia knew that Salim was useful to her. He knew

many things and would be able to guide her in her transition as Zulu's successor. He spoke with so much wisdom, wisdom that could only be gained through experience. She only wondered if she could fully trust him.

"I am loyal to the empire, not the king," he said, reading her mind. "When the tides of power change, my loyalty does as well."

"Good to know," she replied.

Dahlia's mind spun as she rode to the airport with the three-car caravan full of members of the African Mafia trailing behind her. She would have her work cut out for her. Killing Zulu had only been the beginning. Her gender would surely cause many people to doubt her. She would have to rule twice as harshly as Zulu just to be respected half as much. Her mind switched gears as she thought of seeking revenge against Liberty and Po. They seemed like a small problem in the grand scheme of things. She would eventually make them pay for crossing her, but first she had to gain the power that she so desperately sought. If she filled Zulu's seat, she would undoubtedly take over the underworld. Her reach would be endless. As she entered the airport with thirty goons around her, she felt like a queen. They were her protection, they were her minions. There was no way she was going to allow Ali Akban to knock her off of her inherited throne. He was a ghost as far as the game was concerned, and he would remain one. If he showed up, Dahlia was determined to reunite him with his dear friend Zulu.

Dahlia was escorted through a special security line.

Salim had diplomatic status and was treated as a foreign politician when he traveled to the States. They bypassed the crowds and were escorted to the private jet that awaited them. As Dahlia ascended the steps, she took it all in. This was what she had been waiting for. This was the power that she had chased for years, and now she had finally tasted it. She knew in her heart that once she returned to the motherland, nothing in her life would ever be the same. She was about to be initiated into the African Mafia.

SEVEN

AWKWARD SILENCE FILLED THE INTERIOR OF THE car as Liberty, Rocko, and Po made their way across the country. Driving to Detroit was a day-and-a-half trip, including brief stops, and the tension of their past relationships made the hike miserable. As they made their way east across the Nevada desert, the overwhelming heat infiltrated the car. Even the air conditioning wasn't enough to keep them completely cool. The elephant in the room left little space for conversation, and Liberty wanted nothing more at the moment than to escape the confines of the car.

"Pull over," she whispered. They were the first words that had been spoken in four hours. They had been riding together for hundreds of miles with distrust and resentment filling the air. No one slept; everyone was on alert. It was as if they were enemies with a common foe instead of friends.

Po pulled off at the next exit and slowly rolled into the service station.

"Next stop isn't for a while. What we need, we have to buy it here. I'm going to fill up," he said.

Liberty nodded and watched as Po exited the car. Rocko stared out the passenger window, looking in the side-view mirror at his own reflection. His brooding mood could be felt all the way in the backseat.

"You're disappointed in me," Liberty whispered. "Because I forgave Po?"

"You sure you did that?" Rocko replied. "You ain't said two words to him since we got on the road."

Liberty knew that her distance came from being caught between two men. Despite the fact that Po had apologized, she still felt a spark with Rocko. She was attracted to Po's best friend. She had no words for Po, because she was too busy thinking about what she wished she could say to Rocko.

"I don't want you to be mad at me," Liberty said. Her eyes stayed glued to the interior of the service station as she watched Po move around inside.

"I'm good, ma. As long as you're happy, I'm cool with it," Rocko stated.

"You're not cool with it, Rocko," Liberty countered. "And it's OK, because honestly, all I've thought about since we kissed is you. I just don't know what I'm supposed to do. We both know that you and I can't happen."

"We both know it, but it's clear that we don't like it," Rocko replied. "It is what it is, ma. Let's just get to Detroit and get back to what it was. As long as the money's flowing, I'm good. I don't lose focus over women. You don't have to worry about me. I'm not sticking around, anyway.

As soon as we get back to Detroit, I'm done with Po. I got love for him, but our partnership has run its course. I can't get money with a nigga that tried to murk me. The trust will never be the same. Me being here makes things uncomfortable. It's time for me to do my own thing."

Before she could respond, Po got back into the car. His presence immediately silenced the conversation. Liberty's heart grew heavy because she had so much to say. She wanted to make sure that things were right with Rocko. It seemed as if he was withdrawing from her, and the thought that he wouldn't be around once they reached their destination caused her great distress.

"I think I should clean Rocko's wound and change the dressing. We also need Tylenol. He won't be able to rough out the pain for the entire trip," Liberty said softly.

"I'm good," Rocko stated.

"I think Lib is right, Rock. The next exit is at least two hours away," Po said.

Rocko nodded, and Liberty slid out of the backseat. Rocko exited the car on crutches.

"We'll be right back," Liberty said to Po, who nodded as they began to walk away.

Liberty went into the station and rummaged through the shelves until she found everything she needed. She then exited and walked around the building where the restrooms were located. Opening the door, she found Rocko waiting inside. With the click of a lock, they were cloaked in privacy. As she stared at him, she almost forgot that Po was waiting just outside at the gas pump.

"Rocko," she whispered. She closed the distance between them. He leaned against the wall for support as she threw her arms around his neck. She hugged him tightly. "I don't want you to leave," she whispered. "I need you to stick around."

He placed his hand on her abdomen and pushed her away slightly, creating a small space between them. He grimaced as his gunshot wound throbbed intensely.

"Sit down, Rocko. Let me change your dressings," she said.

Rocko lowered the toilet cover, sat on top of it, and extended his leg to her. Liberty got on her knees. "You ain't got to take care of me, ma, that ain't your job." Liberty's hands worked efficiently as she removed, cleaned, and replaced the bloody gauze.

"Rocko, just because Po is back in my life doesn't mean I don't want you to be. Before all of this, we barely spoke. I didn't know you. I'd like to consider you a friend. I need one of those these days," she whispered. "Please stick around, Rocko. You are beginning to mean the world to me, and I just want us to be OK. Are we OK?" she asked.

"He don't deserve you, Liberty," Rocko whispered.

"I know," Liberty replied. "But he needs me, and he needs you. We need each other, Rocko. He is lost right now. How can we preach loyalty to him and be disappointed that he betrayed us if we turn around and do the same thing to him?"

If anyone else had presented it to him, Rocko would have walked away. As a man, he didn't feel he owed another man anything. But this new admiration of a woman made him feel indebted to her. He knew that there wasn't anything that Liberty asked of him that he would say no to. He would stay simply because she had asked him to.

"You're right," he replied.

"You won't leave?" she asked.

"I won't leave you, ma," he answered.

Liberty's smile lit up the entire room as she grabbed Rocko's hand and squeezed it tightly.

"I don't know how to be around you and not crave you, ma," he admitted. He lowered his head as if it truly hurt him. "You did something to me."

"I showed you that you're worth loving, Rocko, and someday a really good woman is going to love you," she replied. A faint smile graced her lips as she stopped talking. Sadness conquered her gaze. She knew that she wanted so much more than a friendship with Rocko. She felt the same connection to him that she had with A'shai. She was just too cowardly to let go of Po. "I'm saying everything I'm supposed to say here, Rocko, but it's not registering in my heart."

"I don't want politically correct, Liberty, I want the truth," Rocko said.

Tears misted in her eyes. "The truth is, I want you, but I can't let Po go. I can't walk away from him to be with his best friend. It's not right. We were supposed to be parents together. He saved me from Samad. I just can't abandon him the way that he tried to do me, but that doesn't stop me from wanting to kiss you right now."

Boom! Boom!

Two strong knocks vibrated against the bathroom door, and they both knew that it was time to check back into reality. She stood sadly and walked to the door to allow Po to enter.

"I'll be in the car," she said as she walked past Po. Po grabbed her wrist and gently pulled her back to him. "Hey. You OK?"

She nodded as he massaged her shoulder reassuringly. "I'm fine."

He pulled her in for a kiss, but she turned her head so that it landed on her cheek. She glanced back at Rocko, then placed two hands on Po's chest. She pushed him off of her gently. She handed him the Tylenol. "He's in some pain. Make sure he takes these. I'll be waiting in the car."

Liberty hurried out of the bathroom and sank into the backseat of the car. She didn't know what to do, but she knew that under no circumstances was she letting Rocko leave. She wanted him around, even though she knew that they wouldn't be able to stop themselves from crossing that line.

Liberty forgave Po, but she would never forget what he had done to her. She kept his betrayal locked away in the back of her mind, but she knew that she had to move forward and attempt to salvage whatever pieces of their relationship were left. Liberty knew that right now, she, Rocko, and Po had to stick together. They needed one another, whether they wanted to admit it or not. Liberty felt obligated to Po as if she owed him something. Despite her feelings for Rocko, she couldn't leave Po, and she couldn't let Rocko leave, either. They were all they had, and she was slowly realizing that she cared for both men for different reasons. They were completely different, and she needed both of them.

After a two-day road trip, they finally arrived at their destination. Liberty, Po, and Rocko were within the city limits of Detroit. It was awkward, because although they rode together, none of them said a word. They all knew that they were bonded for inexplicable reasons. They were forced to be family, and nothing could change that. They were all ready to start a new life in Detroit and let the past stay exactly where it was—in the past. As they neared Liberty's Detroit home, she began to remember why she had left the city. The place reminded her too much of A'shai, and a thick sadness invaded her heart as memories of him came rushing back to her.

Liberty looked out the window. Her heart began to race as they neared the house that A'shai had purchased for her. She smiled, thinking about how he had made sure she had a house that was paid off in full. He always acted as her protector and provider. He was there whenever she needed him, and it seemed as if ever since he had passed, her world wasn't the same. She looked toward the front seats and glanced at Po.

Can I trust him after he betrayed me for Dahlia? Fool me once, shame on him. But fool me twice, shame on me, she thought as she analyzed the current situation. She had offered her home to Po and Rocko just until they settled back into the flow of the streets of Detroit. She really wanted them to do well and thought that was the least she could do. She was willing to work on her relationship with Po, but she didn't want to jump in headfirst. They would live separately, until she decided otherwise. She was only allowing Po to stay in her home until he could make other arrangements. She would never allow another man to claim the home that she shared with A'shai. Liberty knew that the duffel bag of money she had would only last her for so long. She would need Rocko and Po to get by until she could figure out her next move. *Maybe I'll go to school*, she thought, trying to piece a plan together in her mind.

"Make a right up here," Liberty said when she sat up and saw that the street was coming up. Po followed her instructions and turned onto the street. Rocko was impressed with the suburban area. Liberty pointed to her home, and a cold chill overcame her. She saw that the lawn had grown wildly, and the house didn't have the curb appeal that it once possessed. Po pulled into the driveway and threw the car into park. He looked in the rearview mirror at Liberty's face. He saw the pain in her eyes and wanted to comfort her, but he could not find the right words to say to her.

"Give me a minute, guys. I won't be long at all. I want to go in by myself first," she said as she pulled the house keys from her purse and opened the car door. She headed to the house and up to the front door. She slowly slid the key in and turned the lock. *Click clock!* As the sound of the deadbolt unlocking filled the air, her heart began to race. She took a deep breath and walked in. The sounds of her heels hit the hardwood floor as she looked around. She noticed a pile of mail on the floor that had been put through the mail chute in the door. Liberty bent over to pick up the letters. As she examined them, she noticed that they were all addressed to her but had no return addresses.

"These are all in the same handwriting," she whispered to herself as she sifted through the numerous letters. She began to walk through the ice-cold home, remembering when it was filled with love and warmth. She would never forget that feeling.

She looked around the house that she once shared with A'shai and got a weird feeling. She hadn't been to the house in years. The last time she was there, she was grieving the death of the love of her life. She slowly began to walk through the house, and it seemed as if everything in it triggered a memory that she and A'shai had shared. She kept thinking back on that horrible morning, when she woke up to see the man she loved dead beside her. Liberty began to tear up and quickly clenched her teeth and smiled, trying to remember the good times, rather than the one bad one.

Just as she began to open one of the letters, she heard someone walking from the rear of the house. She froze in fear and shot a look in the direction of the sound. The face she saw blew her mind. Her knees buckled, and she put her hand over her mouth. "Oh, my God," she whispered to herself as she locked eyes with a man she hadn't seen in years.

EIGHT

BARON MONTGOMERY LOOKED DOWN AT THE TOMBSTONE, and his heart ached at the sight. He read his son's name carved into the marble stone, and an involuntary tear dropped from his left eye. It haunted him that he could not attend his son's funeral a couple of years back, but his most-wanted status had prevented him from returning to the United States. He had to pay his respects years later. He had snuck back into the country after evading the feds and hiding in seclusion. He had grown a heavy beard and dyed it jet-black. His new appearance was a far cry from the distinguished salt-and-pepper beard he used to wear. It was seldom that you caught Baron Montgomery without an Italian custom suit on, but on this day, he was clad in a basic sweatsuit with dark shades that concealed his eyes. He looked nothing like he did when he was in his prime a couple of years back. He was totally incognito.

"Son, I'm pained that I wasn't there for you when you

needed me most. I am ashamed and wish I could trade places with you." Baron quickly wiped away the tears and looked around the cemetery. He stood there alone. The only sounds were birds chirping and the ruffling of leaves that the wind had stirred up. Baron just couldn't grasp the fact that A'shai had committed suicide. He wanted to know what drove him to such a harsh end. He knew that the only person who could provide the true reason to him was Liberty. He understood deep in his heart that she held all the answers to his questions. He knew that he was somewhat to blame for his family falling apart. His wife was murdered, and his only son was gone. His heavy grief slowly began to shift into guilt as he thought about the illegal life he chose. He could have been a doctor, a lawyer, or even a legit businessman. However, he chose to move heavy amounts of drugs. He had been at the top of the drug-dealing totem pole in his prime, but none of that mattered now. He was wanted by the FBI, he had no family, and none of his street credibility could make this right.

"I'm so sorry, son. I'm so sorry," he whispered as he broke down crying like a baby. He dropped to his knees and placed his forehead on A'shai's tombstone. Baron began to have a flashback of the first time he met his adopted son. He slowly closed his eyes and drifted down memory lane.

Fifteen years ago . . .

Baron held hands with his beautiful young wife as they slowly strolled the edge of the beach. White sand crept in between their toes as the sun's beams smiled down upon them. Willow, young and beautiful, was only thirty years of age and had traveled all around the world with her husband over the years. To say that theirs was a wonderful life was an understatement. She latched onto his arm and hugged it tightly. It was the eve of their anniversary, and she was the happiest woman in the world. Their annual trip to Tijuana was always one of her favorite times of the year. For her, it was complete pleasure. On the other hand, Baron made this trip yearly for two reasons: one, to celebrate years of marriage with his wife, and two, to meet his coke supplier.

Baron was in his early thirties but had managed to become one of the biggest drug suppliers in the U.S. He had a direct connection to the Mexican cartel and purchased the top grade of cocaine for the cheapest prices. The Garza family was one of the biggest cocaine manufacturers in the world, and their import and export operation was worldwide. Baron looked down at his wife, and she peeked up at him, giving him the prettiest smile she could muster.

"I love you, Mr. Montgomery," she said.

"I love you more, sweetheart. I have a surprise for you tomorrow," he said as he returned the smile.

"Oh, yeah? What is it?" she asked, getting noticeably excited.

Baron let out a sly chuckle and shook his head. "If I told you, it wouldn't be a secret, now, would it?" he asked. They both laughed and continued their stroll down the beach, admiring the beautiful scenery.

Willow's life was perfect. She only desired one thing, and that was to have a child for Baron. The doctor had let her know years ago that she was unable to have children. That news had crushed her world, but Baron tried to compensate by spoiling her with gifts and trips across the world. It helped, but the lavish things couldn't fill the void of a child of their own. Baron thought about that void, held her closer, and promised himself he would take the first step and suggest adoption when they returned home. However, he had to take care of business in the meantime. First thing in the morning, he was scheduled to meet his associate and head of the Garza cartel, Diego Garza.

Children and young adults ranging in age from eight to eighteen were packed into a spacious warehouse, mixing and compressing cocaine from the finest coca leaves in Mexico. It resembled a manufacturing company as the youth worked in the sweatshop. Mexican cartel members paced the floor with automatic assault rifles to keep order. Baron entered the building, accompanied by Diego's henchmen. Baron had been to the warehouse many times, but he hadn't remembered the workers being so young. It took him by surprise, and he instantly got sick to his stomach. Although he kept his cool on the outside, he was disgusted. It just didn't look right to him. Nevertheless, he walked past the workers and headed up the steel stairs that led to the office of the kingpin, Diego.

Diego looked down at the main floor through the wide glass. He smiled sinisterly as he watched a million-dollar operation in the works. Diego was a short, stout, full-blooded Mexican. Tattoos covered his body, and his skin was golden brown, kissed by the sun.

Baron entered the office, and Diego's goons all had pistols in their hands, not trusting Baron. Although Baron had been patted down before entering and posed no immediate threat, Diego's goons stayed on high alert. Baron could feel the tension as always, but all animosity subsided when Diego cracked a smile and extended his hand to his most loyal client.

"Good to see you, my friend," Diego said as he shook Baron's hand and signaled for his goons to leave the room immediately.

"Likewise. How are you, Diego?" Baron asked as he kept a straight face, without a smile.

Baron sat down and clasped his hands while Diego slowly paced the room. Even though Baron had been doing business with Diego for years, he still grew uneasy when he came over to discuss brick prices and quantity. There was something about Diego that was sinister and not right, but Baron knew that he was dealing with the best. He needed his coke, not his friendship.

"Baron, how was your flight?" Diego asked, with his back to him as he overlooked his main floor. Diego held both of his hands behind his back, standing tall.

"It was good. Thanks for sending your jet to get the wife and me. We love to visit your beautiful country," Baron responded.

"Yes, it is a beautiful country, isn't it?" Diego said as he glanced back at Baron and released a small grin.

"Indeed."

"So, let's get to business. I know you didn't come over to party and bullshit," Diego said.

Baron rubbed his hands together and prepared to play this game of mental chess. "Absolutely. I want to boost my monthly orders, but I want the price to come down," he said.

"What do you have in mind price-wise?"

"I want to pay five a key," Baron suggested.

Immediately after the price came out of Baron's mouth, a loud laugh erupted. Diego had been giving Baron whole kilos for ten thousand each. Baron had been buying one hundred per month, and he wanted the price to go down because of his loyalty and consistency with his purchases. Baron was a millionaire and had a plan to retire, but he needed to get the prices down on his product to speed up the process.

"Five a key. That's a big difference from what you're paying," Diego said with a smile still on his face.

"I know it's half, but I need more margin for profit. I keep my product pure and at low cost, so I'm not profiting too much off each kilo," Baron said, breaking down the math.

"I can't come down that low on the kilos. However, maybe I could interest you in another type of business," Diego said as he rubbed the hair on his chin. "Let me show you something."

Baron stood up and joined Diego, standing to the right side of him.

"You see that down there? What do you see when you look down there?"

"What do you mean? I see a cocaine factory," Baron said as he looked at Diego in confusion.

"No, look closer," Diego said as he focused his attention on the underage workers. "I see money. In the United

States, there is an underground market for what you are looking at."

"Diego, I'm not fully understanding what you are getting at. What are you talking about?" Baron asked.

"You are inquiring about cocaine to make top dollar when you should be inquiring about those down there," Diego said. His smile turned upside down, and a wave of seriousness came over him. Baron could see the sinister glare in his eyes. Diego looked Baron deep in the eyes and said, "Humans."

"Humans?" Baron asked, thinking that he had heard Diego wrong.

"Yes, my friend. That's where the money is. One person is worth one hundred Gs. The girls we send to the black market brothels in L.A., and sometimes the boys, too. The boys that we keep, we use them to work the fields and make the coke. I have a direct line through Sierra Leone and Haiti," Diego said.

Baron was at a loss for words. His heart dropped when he looked closer and saw how young they were. Human trafficking wasn't his game. The thought of enslaving young boys and girls for profit sickened him. He had no respect for men who participated in the trade, and he now viewed Diego in a different light. He was dealing with the scum of the earth, and Baron promised himself that he would pull out of business with Diego as soon as he was able to locate a new connect. He hid his emotions and looked down at the victims below him. His stomach turned, and his heart ached for them, but it wasn't his place to stop anything. He couldn't save the world, despite the fact that he thought the act of human trafficking was deplorable. Baron's heart was close to the situation, because his wife had once been a part of human trafficking. She would tell him how horrible her childhood was, and he had vowed never to let that happen to her again. So Baron was angered to the tenth power. People like Diego were the same type of people who had scarred his wife for life.

What type of sick, deranged shit is this mu'fucka on? Baron asked himself while keeping a poker face. He knew that he still needed Diego for the coke, and he didn't want to offend him by showing his disgust. "Oh, yeah," Baron said, pretending to be interested.

"Yes, I invested in an import/export boat. They call it the Murderville boat," Diego said proudly, and he rubbed his beard and slowly nodded. "It just looks like an import boat that moves crated goods, but underneath the surface, I'm moving souls. For profit." The look in his eyes resembled the devil himself. He had no compassion for his fellow humans. It was as if he didn't even look at them as people, just product.

Baron clenched his jaws tightly, and his heart began to race. He saw that most of the kids he was looking at shared his skin color, and a deeper issue burned inside him. He was livid. However, he could not show his cards, so he played along. He smiled and nodded as if he was impressed with Diego's business acumen.

"So you are saying you basically have slaves?" Baron asked as his insides were on fire with anger.

"Yes, my friend. If you want to call them that," Diego answered.

"Maybe we can talk about them next trip. Sounds interesting," Baron lied as he rubbed his hands together. He knew that his business with Diego would soon end. He would never be able to sleep at night, knowing that he was doing business with a man of Diego's character.

They agreed on a price for the current shipment, and that was the last time Baron ever saw Diego.

Hours later, Baron and Willow were strolling through the town's market, where the high-end shops were located. Mexico was a beautiful place, and Willow loved shopping there during their vacation.

"Something is on your mind. I can tell," Willow said as she held her husband's hand. Baron looked down at her, smiled, and admired the canary-yellow sundress that she wore.

"Just have a couple of things on my mind, baby. That's all," Baron said with a slight smile. He didn't want to let Willow know, but the images of those children working in the factory tugged at Baron's heart. He couldn't shake the ill feeling he had because of the immoral doings of his business partner.

"Whatever it is, I know it will get better. You always make the right moves and decisions. This I know," Willow said. Baron smiled and shook his head while letting out a light chuckle. Willow smiled and looked up at him. "What's funny?" she asked.

"It's just that no matter the situation, you always say the right things and make it better. Even when you don't know what the problem is," Baron said.

"I know, I'm good, right?" Willow said playfully. They both laughed, and Willow looked through the window of a jewelry store. She stopped and marveled at the handcrafted jewelry on display.

"Oh, my God. This is so beautiful," Willow said as she placed her hand on her mouth in awe.

"Why don't you go into the shop and check it out? I have to use the bathroom, anyway." Baron said as he spotted a restroom sign in the strip mall across the walkway.

"OK, great. I'll be inside."

Willow entered the shop, and Baron walked across the street, leaving his wife alone.

The boys hid behind the oversized dumpster and watched as the wealthy American tourists walked the small strip of shops. They were looking for a mark who seemed to have money so that they could snatch a bag or purse. The field workers would do this every weekend, in hopes of hitting a jackpot. A'shai was the youngest of the boys, but he was the fastest, so they usually made him do the actual snatching.

"You see those diamonds?" the eldest said as they saw a beautiful woman come out of one of the shops. She was dipped in diamonds and blinged as the sun hit her ring, bracelet, and necklace. She was fair-skinned, and her slim body was perfect. She looked as if she could be a famous supermodel, and with the kind of jewelry she had on, maybe she was.

"Shai, she is the one. I bet you she has tons of money in de' purse," the Haitian boy said in a heavy accent.

"I got it. I got it," Shai said as he stared down the potential victim.

He nodded his head as he rubbed his hands together, waiting for the right time. He came from behind the dumpster and began to walk toward her. Shai put his hands in his pockets, trying to look as natural as possible as he neared the unsuspecting woman. His heart began to beat fast as he approached the woman, who held her purse in one hand and a shopping bag in the other. He felt the adrenaline kick in, and that's when he went for it. He ran up to the lady, snatched both bags from her hands, and took off toward the alley where his accomplices were waiting.

"Hey! Come back here!" the lady yelled just before she pulled off her stilettos and gave chase.

Shai was running full speed as the boys cheered him on, but he stepped in a pothole in the road and twisted his ankle. He grimaced in pain and hobbled to the alley. Once he reached the alley, the lady had caught up with him and grabbed him by the back of his collar. The other boys emerged from behind the dumpster.

"Well, hello there, pretty gal," one Haitian field worker said as he circled the lady.

"I just want my things back," she said, releasing her grip on A'shai.

The Haitian boy began to fondle the woman, grabbing her butt and laughing as the other boys began to circle her. Shai stepped back, not knowing what was going on. He just wanted her belongings, nothing more, nothing less.

"What you want to give me for de' purse?" the Haitian boy asked as he looked at her with lustful eyes. He was the leader, so the other boys followed suit and began to touch the lady inappropriately. She cringed and stepped back, trying to avoid the young boy's touch.

"You can have the purse. I just want to leave," the woman pleaded, backing down as she tried to exit the alley.

The Haitian boy jumped into her path, stopping her. "Why you rushing off? Let's have some real fun," he said as he grabbed his crotch and laughed sinisterly.

"Yo, what the fuck is going on? Let her go," Shai said as he realized their intentions. He didn't want to sexually assault the woman in any form or fashion.

"Stop being a pussy, Shai," another boy said as he stepped forward.

"Let's just take the purse and go, man," Shai pleaded. The other boys had already planned what they were going to do to the American beauty, and they weren't letting Shai get in the way. Two of the boys grabbed Shai and held him back while the other two began to forcefully rip off the woman's clothes. "Let her go!" Shai screamed as he tried to shake loose from their grasp. They were much too strong for Shai's small frame. They managed to rip the woman's shirt completely off, exposing her breasts, and they muffled both her and Shai's mouths as they prepared to rape her. The woman looked at

Shai, and both of them had tears in their eyes, knowing what heinous act was about to happen.

There was a brief moment of silence just before the big boom. The sound of a gun being blasted echoed through the alleyway, and blood splattered against the brick wall along with the young Haitian boy's brains. A tall, slender black man stood holding the gun, with a cigar hanging from his mouth. He was dark and well-built and sported a three-thousand-dollar suit. Everyone jumped at the sound of the blast. There stood Baron with a gun in his hand. He quickly grabbed up the other boy who was abusing his wife and flung him like a rag doll against the building. Rage was evident all over Baron's face. The other kids tried to get away, but Baron let off another round into the air.

"If anybody moves, I'm blowing their fucking heads off! Everybody get against the fucking wall," he demanded. His eyes were bloodshot-red as his blood boiled with anger. He only saw red at that point. He knelt down and helped his wife up. "Are you OK, Willow?" he asked as he took off his jacket and covered her up. She shook her head yes as she wiped her tears away. "I want you to see something, baby," he whispered as he ran his hand through her hair and gave her a kiss to the forehead.

"Line up against the wall," Baron ordered as he turned his attention to the remaining three boys, including Shai. He walked over to them and took a puff of his cigar. He then dropped it to the ground and stepped on it. "Do you know who the fuck I am?" he asked one of the young boys as he stood in front of him. Before the boy could answer, Baron pointed the gun to his head and squeezed the trigger, rocking him to sleep forever. His blood and brains splattered against the wall, his body fell limp, and he eventually collapsed facedown. Shai and the last boy were petrified as they began to plead, but Baron didn't care. He put the gun to Shai's head and told him, "If you believe in God, you better pray to him right now. Say your peace." He tightened his grip on the gun.

"Baron, wait! He tried to help me. It was the others who tried to rape me. Leave him be," his wife said.

"Are you sure?" he asked, looking back at her.

"Yeah, I'm positive. He was the one trying to stop them," she said as she looked into Shai's young eyes.

Baron then pointed his gun at the other boy and fired two shots into his chest with no remorse. He put the smoking gun in his waistband and looked at Shai, whose knees were trembling.

"Thanks for what you did for my wife, li'l man," Baron said, smiling to ease the kid's fear. He reached into his pocket, pulled out five crispy bills, and handed them to Shai.

Shai waved his hand, rejecting the offer. "I'm good. I didn't like these mu'fuckas, anyway," he said as he looked down at their bodies. "Can I go?"

"Yeah, you can go." Baron grinned at the wit of the youngster who stood before him.

A'shai turned around and headed down the alley so that he could return to the fields. Baron and his wife watched him walk away. However, something in Willow's heart told her to stop him.

"Hey!" she called out. A'shai stopped and turned around.

"Let us buy you dinner," she said, feeling that she had to repay him for his bravery in going against his friends for her honor.

Free food was too good an offer for Shai to let pass, and he headed back their way.

Baron and Willow watched as the kid stuffed his face as if it would be his last meal. Four different entrees were in front of him as they encouraged him to order anything he wanted. A'shai didn't once look up and think about how barbaric he looked in front of total strangers. The restaurant was the most elegant one in Tijuana's downtown resort. A'shai had never seen anything like it, and the food was the best he had ever had. He had already stuffed four rolls into his pocket, knowing that they would come in handy later.

"Slow down," Willow said, and she burst into laughter. She looked at Baron, and he also was laughing at the young boy, and that's when Shai finally looked up. He had sauce all around his mouth and on his fingertips as he ate the food like a madman.

"What?" A'shai asked as an odd moment of silence filled the air. Baron and Willow just looked at him, both with grins on their faces.

"Nothing. So tell me, where are your parents?" Baron asked as he folded his hands on top of the table.

A'shai focused back on his food and began to eat. "I don't have any parents," he said, thinking about his deceased mother and his estranged father back in Sierra Leone. "I don't need any parents. I can take care of myself." He avoided eye contact with Baron.

"I can tell that you're not from around here. Your accent is too strong," Baron said, noticing the strong African roots in the boy.

"I'm from Sierra Leone!" A'shai said proudly as he stuck out his chest and looked at Baron with clenched teeth.

Willow's heart immediately dropped, because that was her homeland; she, too, was from the impoverished country. She reached over and touched the scar on A'shai's face. "How did you get that?" she asked, hoping not to hear a horror story.

"It's nothing. Just a little scratch," A'shai said as he blew it off. He began to grow uncomfortable with all of the questions, and then he noticed that the sun was going down. He knew that he had to return to the warehouse before dark or risk being whipped or beaten. "Thank you for giving me dinner. But I have to go now," he said urgently, and stood up. The thought of being late and getting whipped made his limbs shake, and he grew nervous.

Baron caught on. "Are you OK, li'l man?" he asked, frowning at the sudden change of behavior.

"Yeah, I just have to go before they notice that I'm gone," A'shai said.

Willow began to tear up as she thought about her childhood. She, too, was a human slave as a teen but was lucky enough to have met Baron. Willow knew that A'shai was in the same boat she had been in years ago.

Baron also picked up on it. "Listen, do you work for the Garza family? You can tell me," he said as he stood up and walked around the table in front of A'shai.

A'shai nodded his head yes.

"He is an old friend of mine. We should go have a talk with him," Baron said as he placed his hand on A'shai's shoulder.

They left the restaurant and headed over to the Garza warehouse. A'shai told them the truth about how he got to Tijuana, and it nearly brought both Willow and Baron to tears. They decided at that point that A'shai would return to the States with them. They had no children of their own, and it was as if fate brought them to A'shai. Willow, because of the earlier sexual abuse, was unable to have kids, so she was open to taking in A'shai. The fact that A'shai was from her homeland made it even more special to her. He connected Willow to her roots, and Baron understood that. When he looked into A'shai's eyes, he saw the eye of the tiger.

They both fell in love with Shai in that brief meeting, and the rest was history. A'shai was on Baron's private jet back to Detroit with them that night. He had been one of the lucky ones.

NINE

BARON SNAPPED BACK TO REALITY AS HE looked down at A'shai's tombstone. His flashback was so vivid, so real. At that point, tears were pouring down. The thoughts of all he had lost over the years seemed to come crashing down on him. He had lost his wife, his only son, his place as king in the streets. He was reduced to being a wanted fugitive with nothing left but memories. He tapped his shoulders, his forehead, and his stomach to resemble a cross, sending prayers above. He hoped that both Willow and A'shai were resting in peace. Then the thoughts of how A'shai left the world began to bother him again.

He really wished he could have been there to coach him through whatever dilemma he was going through. He couldn't understand why A'shai would have killed himself. *He was so strong. It just doesn't make sense,* he thought as he wiped his tears away and shook his head in disbelief. He believed suicide was for the weak, and he knew for a fact that A'shai was one of the strongest human beings he had ever met. Things just didn't add up. He needed answers, and he knew where he could directly get them. He needed desperately to see Liberty for closure. For the past few years, he had sent her letters, but he had gotten no response. He knew that he would soon have to return to hiding, so time was of the essence. He was on a mission to find the only person who truly knew what had happened with his dead son.

It was Baron's first time in the States since he went on the run from the feds, so he was determined to pay her a visit. *I just pray to God she is in same house that A'shai purchased.* He was about to give it a try. He had sent numerous discreet letters to Liberty, requesting her to come see him. However, she never showed up. Baron took a deep breath, looked around, and put on the cap he had in his back pocket. Pulling the cap low to cover his eyes, he headed to the house in search of Liberty. He had to know what drove his son to take his own life.

Baron approached the house, and from the outside, it seemed as if it had been abandoned for years. The grass was at knee's length, notices were posted on the front door, and weeds surrounded the home. It was obvious that no one lived there, and it seemed as if all of Baron's hope went out the window. He was really hoping that Liberty still resided at the home. He would have to start from square one to locate her, but he was up for the task. He stepped out of the Honda Civic that he had purchased in Texas from a shady car dealership. He walked toward the house, and a thought popped into his head. He remembered that when Shai was younger, he had a bad habit of losing his keys, so he always kept a spare in the back under a rug. Baron knew it was a long shot, but nobody knew his son like he did, and he had a hunch to go check the back of the house. Baron looked around and then made his way to the back of the house. He saw a rug by the back door and walked toward it. He lifted the rug, and just like he had figured, a single key lay underneath it. Baron laughed to himself and looked up at the sky as if Shai could see him.

"Boy, I know yo' ass like the back of my hand," he said as he shook the key and smiled. Baron then proceeded to unlock the back door. The key fit perfectly, and within seconds, he was inside the house. He slowly walked in, scanning from left to right. The place was fully furnished, but it was freezing cold. He walked on the creaky hardwood floors and knew that it had been empty for quite a while. There was a coldness to the house that told a story in itself. As Baron made his way into the living room, he stopped in his tracks when he saw a picture on the mantel. His heart instantly dropped. It was a picture that he, Willow, and A'shai had taken on the first night he came home with them. A'shai cherished that photo because it was the day his life was changed forever. However, A'shai never knew that Baron's and Willow's lives had been changed that day, too. A'shai brought so much joy into their lives, and they had never known that something was missing until A'shai's love showed them by filling the void.

Baron slowly walked over to the mantel and picked

up the framed photo. He smiled, thinking about the good times that they had shared. He then went to the back of the house and to the bedroom. He looked at the master bed and began to think about the coroner's report. A'shai's death had been labeled a suicide. Baron knew in his heart that A'shai had used the black tea recipe to end his own life. It was a recipe that Baron had taught him. Grief filled him as he ran his hand across the bed, noticing another picture on the nightstand. That picture was of A'shai and Liberty. They were smiling. It was the happiest that Baron had ever seen his son. A'shai's smile made Baron feel warm inside. Just as Baron cracked a smile, he heard a noise in the front room. He instantly tensed up and reached for his gun. If it was the feds, he was going out shooting. He refused to go to prison, so he would be prepared to go all out. He put down the pictures and eased his way to the living room.

He slowly walked in and found himself staring into the face that he was looking for. It was Liberty. She jumped in fear and placed her hands on her chest. She dropped the letters that she had in her hand, and she was at a loss for words. She didn't know what to say or do. She hadn't seen Baron in years, and the last time she remembered, he didn't care for her too much. There was an uncomfortable silence as they stared at each other, saying nothing. Baron was the first to break the silence as he slowly stepped toward her.

"Hello, Liberty," Baron said as he slid his gun back into his waistband. His eyes were kind, so Liberty relaxed.

"Hello, Mr. Montgomery," Liberty said with a shaky voice. She didn't know what to expect from him. Baron put her at ease by smiling and opening his arms. Liberty fell into his arms and gave him a big hug.

"How are you?" he asked as they unlocked their embrace.

"I'm OK," she answered. "You look different," she added as she looked him up and down. She had never seen Baron in less than the finest Italian-cut threads or a suit. His facial hair was thick, and he looked like a shell of himself.

"We have a lot to talk about," Baron said.

Liberty nodded in agreement and made her way over to the couch. "Yes, we do," she said.

Baron rubbed his hands together and blew on them to try to create some heat. Liberty made herself comfortable on the couch and suggested that Baron light the furnace in the basement.

"Where is a lighter?" he asked. Liberty pointed him to the china cabinet, and Baron grabbed the lighter and headed to the basement.

Liberty sat on the couch nervously, knowing that Baron would ask her about A'shai's death. Nevertheless, she was ready to talk. He needed to know what really happened.

While Baron was in the basement, a small knock sounded at the door. Liberty stood up to see who it was. Rocko and Po were standing there. She had totally forgotten about them being outside waiting for her.

"I got to take a leak," Po said as he stepped in and looked around the place. Rocko also stepped in.

Liberty pointed toward the back where the bathroom was. "First door to the right," she said. Liberty returned to the couch and watched as Po headed toward the back.

Rocko walked around the house and began to look at some of the pictures of A'shai and her.

"So this was him, huh?" he asked as he remembered the stories Liberty had told him about the love of her life.

"Yeah, that's A'shai. He was my everything," she replied proudly.

Just as Rocko was about to answer, Baron emerged from the basement. Rocko instantly put his hand to his waist where his gun was located. Baron did the same.

Liberty quickly interjected. "Guys! Relax!" she shouted as she walked in between them with her hands up. That's when Po reentered the room in the middle of the chaos.

"Liberty, what's going on here?" Baron asked.

"Everyone, please calm down!" Liberty yelled. "Let me make the proper introductions. This is Po and Rocko. They came into my life after A'shai passed away. Po and Rocko, this is—" Liberty started to say, but Po interrupted her.

"Baron Montgomery," Po said, finishing her sentence for him. He looked at Baron in complete admiration. He remembered the gangster stories about Baron growing up. Po was a Detroit native, so he grew up idolizing the street legend known as Baron Montgomery. Baron's name rang bells in the streets, and he single-handedly ran Detroit's drug game and political game for years. He was known as the mayor of Detroit in his heyday. Po was staring into the eyes of a person whom he once aspired to be. Po was the first to extend his hand out of respect. Baron didn't acknowledge Po. He just looked at his hand and stepped past him as if he wasn't even there.

"May I talk to you in the living room?" Baron asked Liberty, while Po's hand lingered in the air.

"Sure," Liberty answered, looking at Po and Rocko.

"Look, ma, I'm sure y'all have a lot to talk about. We are going to check into a hotel. Call if you need me," Po said as he put his hands down.

Rocko looked at Po as if he was crazy. Rocko didn't know who Baron was and was ready to put hands on him. Rocko was a stone-cold killer, and at the moment, he was eager to put in work. He already had to contain his resentment toward Po. He needed to release some frustration, and Baron was testing him, and the disrespect had him ready to rock a nigga to sleep. Rocko had an ice-cold grille, and Po placed his hand on his shoulder, signaling him to calm down. Po understood that they were dealing with an OG, and there were rules to the game that Po had to follow. He would explain to Rocko who Baron was later.

"Yo, let's go," Po said as he headed toward the door. Rocko followed Po out, but not before giving Baron a menacing stare as he passed him.

Baron chuckled to himself as he returned the stare and watched them leave. He waited until they were completely out before he focused his attention back on Liberty.

"I don't care about your current situation with these men. They are not my concern. Honestly, I just want to know what happened with my son," Baron said, cutting straight to the point.

"He . . ." Liberty began to say before her voice started to crack. Just the thought alone made her weak. "He promised me that we would die old together. He took his life to be with me . . ." She began breaking down in tears.

Baron walked over and comforted her. They sat on the couch and began to talk. Liberty broke down everything to Baron, telling him what all had happened and getting him up to speed. They sat and talked well into the night, which also acted as a cleansing of Liberty's soul. She also told him about Po and Dahlia. She left no stone unturned.

Baron listened closely and comforted Liberty. He felt obligated to help her. He felt that she was the closest thing to family he had left.

TEN

"HOW FAR OUTSIDE OF THE CITY IS Zulu's home?" Dahlia complained as she watched the African countryside pass by outside her window. She could see the heat waves rising from the dry land. It was dangerously hot, making for an uncomfortable ride. Even the truck's air conditioning couldn't completely combat the temperature.

"Two hundred miles," Salim replied. "It is a precaution that Zulu took. He never let any outsiders know where he rested his head at night."

Dahlia nodded as she sat back in the chauffeured SUV. Her patience was thin as anxiety filled her. If Ali Akban did come back to Sierra Leone, she wanted to be prepared for him. There would be no way that Ali would not seek out his old flame. Dahlia would ensure that Harrah was on her side when Ali decided to reunite. Dahlia was prepared to force Harrah's hand by any means necessary. She wasn't looking to be loved as a leader. Love would get you killed . . . love would leave room for betrayal. That is why wives who loved their husbands still cheated. But the wives who feared their husbands remained strangely loyal, never bucking against the men they feared. Dahlia would rule like a tyrant, and because of that, she would be in control, with no threat of opposition. Her head spun as she weighed the new responsibilities that sat on her shoulders, but on the outside, she remained cool and composed as she watched the native land swirl by. Dusk gave way to the night, and everything went black outside her window. It was as if someone had shut off the lights suddenly, cloaking the vehicle in darkness. In the distance, she saw yellow lights shining. She knew that it was Zulu's home. It was so out of place, built up like a kingdom in the middle of nowhere. It seemed to take forever for the driver to close the distance. Finally, they arrived. She was escorted by two additional trucks. Like being the president, her new role came with protection. Four goons stepped out of the truck in front of her and four out of the one behind her. She stepped out and looked up at Zulu's home. The massiveness of it all took her breath away. Zulu had truly built himself a castle.

The men gathered around her, awaiting their instructions.

"Cover every entrance of this home, and kill everyone inside, except for Zulu's wife," Dahlia stated coldly.

The men dispersed, with AK-47s and various hand-guns, as Dahlia and Salim walked calmly toward the front entrance. It was stormed first by the goons, who kicked in the door before spilling into the house. Dahlia followed and watched as chaos erupted. Housekeepers and the armed guards Zulu had left behind were surprised as gunfire erupted.

RAT TAT TAT TAT TAT TAT!

The bullets ripped through everything in the front room as Dahlia stood calmly behind the sparks of the rapid fire. She raised her hand to signal a cease fire when she saw one of the men dragging Zulu's wife down the spiral staircase. Dahlia watched, slightly mesmerized, as the woman struggled against her captor. Dahlia didn't know what she had expected, but Harrah's beauty was unparalleled. She looked like a real woman, and in a world where hair extensions and a face full of cosmetics dominated beauty, her natural essence was surprising. Her skin was the color of slightly creamed coffee. Her bosom was full and her body slightly round, as if she had feasted on the finest cuisines while sipping wine with the royals for years. Her kinky hair was jet-black and extended outward in a long, untamed halo around her head. When Dahlia looked into her eyes, Harrah's long lashes batted in anger. She was clearly used to being the queen of her castle and didn't appreciate that it had been ransacked. A sense of relief mixed with confusion filled her face when she saw Salim standing behind Dahlia.

"Thank goodness, Salim!" she exclaimed as she snatched her arm away from the goon violently. "Unhand me, you imbecile! What is the meaning of this, Salim? Where is Zulu?"

Salim cleared his throat as he stood with his hands clasped behind his back. He hated to be the one to do this to Harrah. He had known her for many years, back when she was a young woman whom all the local men craved. He had eaten in her home on holidays, seen her through the miscarriages of her children, and watched her evolution from girl to woman. In another realm, they would have been considered friends, but in the world of drugs, diamonds, and money, there was no such thing.

"Zulu is dead," Salim said.

"No." Her voice echoed as she shook her head in disbelief. "No!" It wasn't her love for him that caused her to break on the inside but her dependency on him. There was plenty of money to take care of her financial needs for the rest of her life, but with that much money came the threat of danger. Without Zulu, her protection went out the door, hence the invasion of her home at that very moment. She had been with Zulu since she was a young woman, navigating her way around the world. He was all that she knew. How would she survive alone? She had no friends, no family. Zulu had kept her secluded for years, which had caused everyone she loved to drift away from her. It was just the two of them and the many people who were around because they were paid to be. There was no real love, no real loyalty. Salim was an example of that.

"I assure you, Zulu is dead. I am the one who killed him." Dahlia spoke calmly.

Harrah's eyes widened in complete surprise. None of his adversaries in Africa had been able to touch Zulu. How had he allowed himself to slip at the hands of a female?

"You're here for the money? You can have it. You don't

have to hurt the people who work for me. I will give it to you. The last thing I want is war," Harrah said.

Dahlia chuckled. "I'm not here for the money, Harrah. I am here for you. I seek your assistance. A lot of people can breathe easily now that Zulu is no longer alive. One person in particular, Ali Akban . . ."

Dahlia saw the flicker of hope spark in Harrah as the name rolled off of her tongue.

It had been so long since Harrah had allowed herself to think of him, but with just the mention of his return, all of the feelings that she had buried surfaced. The familiar flutter of butterflies filled her stomach.

"If I know men, and trust me, I do . . ." Dahlia stopped and smirked to herself as she thought of all the men who had fallen victim to her mind games. "Ali will come back here to see if the rumors of Zulu's demise are true. He will want to pick up where Zulu left off, and I can't allow that to happen. When he comes to town, he will undoubtedly come for you first. I heard the two of you had quite the love affair."

Harrah's mouth was straight in a tight mug, and she squared her shoulders as she gave Dahlia a look of contempt. "An affair is dirty. We shared love. I was planning to leave Zulu for him."

"Which is exactly why you are the perfect person to help me kill him," Dahlia concluded.

"I won't," Harrah said firmly.

"How valiant," Dahlia said sarcastically. "But of course you will. It's called self-preservation. Either you help me get to Ali Akban, or I will murder you. You want to make sure you are of use to me. It would be best if you complied."

"I was with Zulu for thirty years. You are as brand new as you look if you think I'm afraid of you. You don't have the balls to kill Zulu's widow," Harrah spat arrogantly. "The heads of the five families would annihilate you for the disrespect alone."

Dahlia nodded, and on cue, the goon standing behind Harrah took her down to the floor, planting a knee in her back.

"You are a stupid little girl!" Harrah shouted, with her hands spread out on the floor. "You have no idea who I am."

"No, I know exactly who you are, Harrah. I just don't give a fuck," Dahlia said. "Zulu's reign is over. His men now follow me. Once I get rid of Ali, the families will back me. So it is you who are clueless, Harrah. You have no idea who *I* am." Dahlia removed a small revolver handgun and opened the chamber. "I have one bullet in this gun. Let's play a little Russian Roulette, eh?" She stepped over Harrah and placed the gun to the back of her head. Dahlia was developing a ruthlessness that not even Zulu had possessed. She could blow Harrah's head off with no regret.

She pulled the trigger. *CLICK!*

"Agh!" Harrah cried out, the torturous weapon of the unknown being used against her.

Dahlia pulled the trigger again. *CLICK!*

"Hmmm!" Harrah flinched, anticipating the shot that would spread her brains across the expensive bamboo flooring.

CLICK!

Harrah was counting the false shots. She was running out of chances to live. Luck was on her side, but it would eventually run out.

CLICK!

Tears fell down her cheeks as fear forced her loyalty to run low. "OK . . ."

CLICK!

"OK!" she screamed, horrified.

"Stand her up," Dahlia commanded. "When Ali tries to contact you, I trust that you will let me know."

Harrah was so full of anger, fear, and confusion that she couldn't look Dahlia in the eyes. "I will."

Dahlia turned for the door. "My men will clean up the mess they made. I'll be in touch," she said. Just before she walked out, she turned and concluded, "Don't run. Prey run. I don't want to have to hunt you, love. After you help me get to Ali, I will disappear from your life as if I had never appeared. Your cooperation is appreciated."

Cold skin. Pale cheeks. Ashen pigment. Zulu lay before Harrah bearing no resemblance to the powerful figure he used to be. Death had dwarfed him. He appeared so small in death. The sight of him sent a chill down her spine. She hid behind the widow's veil as she stood frozen in time. There were no tears. She couldn't focus on mourning, because she was too filled with fear. She knew who sat behind the dark tint of the SUVs parked one hundred yards away on the road. Dahlia was watching her. Those same black trucks stalked her house and followed her into town. Her every move was being watched, just in case Ali made his way back to her. She silently hoped that he would stay away, but she knew in her heart that he wouldn't. Now that Zulu didn't stand between them, Ali would inevitably come running. He was like any other man. He was a king who was lost without a queen, and he had always wanted Harrah. No time or distance could wean him off of her.

Harrah stepped back from the wooden raft that Zulu's body lay on. He wouldn't have a traditional service. Long ago, he had decided that he would be funeralized like a king. He had been very specific with Harrah, explaining to her what to do when he was gone. He always knew that the game would take him away from her when they least expected. She was prepared, and she gave him the home going that he had requested. There would be no grave, no casket, just a king lying on a bed of fire as he drifted off to sea. Harrah took the flaming wooden club and placed it at Zulu's feet. A small fire started, and for the first time, she had to choke back emotion. The heads of the five families stood around her, an entire network of people behind them. Two men walked up and pushed the raft into the river that flowed peacefully in front of them. The group stood in silence as the current carried the burning body downriver.

"He's gone," Harrah whispered to herself. She felt numb to it all. Most widows would feel an extreme emptiness, a void, a sadness in the pit of their soul. Harrah felt . . . free. After decades together, she was finally unbound from the stigma that was Zulu. No longer did she have to consider her husband before she considered herself. As his raft disappeared from sight, she bid her final good-bye and then turned toward the crowd.

"I want to thank all of you for coming to pay your respects. I appreciate you, and I know Zulu would have, too. His true comrades are the ones who showed up today. There is no need to worry about me. I am overwhelmed by the many phone calls, flowers, and gifts that I have received. There will be a dinner in his honor today at the local church. Please head over there now. We will be honoring Zulu. May he rest in peace."

"Rest in peace," the group repeated solemnly.

Harrah stood looking as the people passed her by. Dahlia had been wrong. Ali had not shown up. He was nowhere to be found. A piece of her was filled with disappointment. She had gotten used to the idea of seeing his face again, even if it was only a short reunion thanks to Dahlia's intentions for him. As she walked over to her waiting town car, she passed one of the tinted black SUVs. The back window rolled down, and she saw Dahlia's face. Suddenly, it didn't matter that it was the middle of summer; her entire body chilled to the bone.

"Our arrangement still stands. When Ali Akban contacts you, you contact me. Are we clear?"

"We're clear," she responded bitterly.

Dahlia rolled the window up abruptly, ending the conversation. Harrah watched as the truck rolled away. She was so nervous that knots formed in her abdomen. She didn't know what would happen if Ali never showed. She and Dahlia had not even spoken of the possibility. Harrah retreated to the safety of her own ride, stepping into the backseat as the driver held the door open for her. It felt as if someone had a vise grip around her heart. How she was able to keep it all together she did not know. On the outside, she was composed and handling all of Zulu's affairs, when really all she wanted to do was run. Run away from Dahlia, run away from the responsibilities that came with being the widow of one of Africa's finest. Harrah just wanted freedom and peace of mind, but Dahlia was making her earn it. Not until after she had done the bidding of a madwoman would she truly be able to move on.

She arrived at the church to find that most of the attendees of Zulu's unconventional funeral were already there. She didn't know how she was supposed to act normally when everything in her life was spiraling out of control. Her jittery nerves were hard to manage. She breathed deeply to steady her racing heart as she stepped out and made her entrance. Sympathetic eyes fell upon her, and the guests offered their condolences as she walked by. It was a large gathering. More than a hundred people filled the room, and Harrah put up her strongest front as she played hostess. Servers in white coats moved swiftly in and out of the kitchen as they ensured that her guests were accommodated. The commotion of it all was too much.

A girl in a server's coat came up to her. "Ma'am, there is an issue in the kitchen," she informed her.

Harrah nodded and made her way across the room. She

pushed open the swinging door and entered the kitchen, only to find that everything seemed to be running smoothly.

"Is there a problem back here?" she asked one of the waiters, who was carrying a platter full of delicacies.

"No, everything is fine, I believe," the young man responded.

Harrah frowned in confusion, and as she turned to exit, she felt a tug at her hand, and she was pulled quickly into a walk-in pantry. A firm hand was quickly placed over her mouth as the door to the pantry was closed, cloaking her in darkness.

"Shhh!"

She heard the click of a light, and suddenly, a small yellow glow illuminated the small space. She found herself looking into the eyes of Ali Akban. He stood before her in a white server's coat like those that flooded the entire party. He put a finger to his lips, and she nodded. He released the firm hold he had on her, and she jumped into his arms, hugging him tightly as a flood of emotions came over her. She cried on his shoulder as he comforted her.

"It's OK, Harrah," he whispered, rubbing her hair while never letting her out of the embrace. "I'm here now."

Harrah thought of the goons she knew were sitting outside the church. They were watching her every move, just waiting for Ali to surface. She thought of telling him, warning him about Dahlia, but did he deserve her loyalty? By going against the grain, she would be putting her life at risk for him. Dahlia would kill her if she ever found out. Was Ali worth it?

"I have so much I want to ask you," she whispered as she peered at him with a mixture of love and hate. As much as he had claimed to love her, he had just left without looking back. He had left her with a bitter Zulu, knowing that the punishment for their affair would be severe. "Where have you been? How could you just leave me here?"

"Zulu didn't give me much of a choice, Harrah. You have to trust me when I say that leaving was the only way that I could truly keep you safe. Zulu was a gangster. He wouldn't have killed me, Harrah. He would have killed you to get to me. I know, because it is what I would have done if I was the one in his position," Ali admitted.

Her eyes narrowed into slits of misunderstanding. "You're not a monster."

"I am a monster, Harrah. You just happen to love me. You do still love me?" Ali posed the question, not wanting to make assumptions.

Harrah knew that she did. She always had, and no matter if she faced certain death, she couldn't see herself handing him over to Dahlia. The memories of years ago were affecting her good judgment. She didn't care if she only had a few hours to love Ali, she was going to.

"We have to get out of here, Ali. It's not safe. There is so much I need to tell you but not here. Meet me at the back door. I'll pull up in five minutes."

Harrah rushed out of the church and walked up to the driver, who stood attentively at the car.

"Please come inside and have dinner with the guests. This will last for quite a while. It isn't necessary for you to spend the evening outside. At least grab a bite to eat, even if you don't want to sit inside," Harrah said. The driver agreed, and Harrah smiled as he passed her, the keys to the car hanging from his back pocket. She discreetly picked them out and waited until he was out of sight before she hijacked the car. She pulled around the building and up to the back door. Ali came out on cue. He hopped inside, and Harrah hurried off, driving as fast as she could, to a destination unknown.

"Hey, Harrah, wait a minute!" Ali yelled after her as she rushed around the hotel room that they had just checked into.

She was frantic as she placed a chair beneath the door handle and then went to the window to pull the curtains closed. "I don't think we were followed," she said.

"Followed by who, Harrah? You're not making sense. Who are you so afraid of?" Ali asked as he watched her, perplexed.

Harrah stopped and sat down on the edge of the bed as she looked up at Ali. "You're in danger, Ali . . . we both are."

He crossed the room and stood between her legs, reaching down to grab her chin and force her to look at him. "What are you saying?" he asked.

"Dahlia, the woman who killed Zulu . . . she wants to kill you. She has taken Zulu's soldiers; even Salim seems to work for her now. It's like she just stepped into his shoes. She came to my home, killed the men Zulu had left behind for my protection. She told me she would let me live if I helped her get to you," Harrah said. "It had been years. I didn't even think that you would return, but here you are standing in front of me. I could never live with myself if I betrayed you. You are the love of my life."

The news of Dahlia's plot against him was disturbing, and he drew back from Harrah slightly as he processed it all. "Dry your eyes, Harrah. This Dahlia woman will not hurt you. Now that I'm here, everything will be fine. She won't be able to hold on to Zulu's spot. The five families will never approve. I'm going to pick up right where I left off, and once I do, she will be the first to go. Don't worry about her. I promise, she only intimidates you because you are vulnerable right now. She is no threat to me," he said.

Harrah was shocked. How could he be so calm? When circumstances seemed so dire, he was always unusually calm. "You don't know what she is capable of." The tremor of her voice revealed her dread.

"I know what I'm capable of," he asserted. He bent down and kissed her lips gently. "I'm back, Harrah, and I won't allow this woman or anyone else to harm you. The fact that you brought me here to warn me shows your loyalty. Even after all these years, you are still so beautiful, inside and out," he stated. "I want you to stay here. Do not leave this room until I come back."

Harrah grasped his hand tightly in panic. "No! You can't leave!"

He gently removed her hand. "I'm going to speak with the five families. Once they realize I'm alive, they won't welcome Dahlia into the fold. She will have no legs to stand on without the African Mafia as support. Then all of what was Zulu's becomes mine . . . including you."

RING! RING!

Confusion filled Harrah's brain as the loud shrill of the hotel phone awakened her from her restless sleep. At first, she thought it might be a dream, but the ringing was non-stop. Harrah rolled over and picked up the receiver.

"Ali," she whispered. She knew that no one else knew where she was. He was the only person who could possibly be calling her.

"Come and meet me at our spot," Ali replied.

She looked at the red numbers on the digital clock beside her. "It's four in the morning," she said. "Now?"

"Yes, now. Come and run away with me, Harrah. We don't have to stay here in Sierra Leone. With Zulu's money, we can leave and never look back. I left the car downstairs. Take it, and meet me now," he urged.

"What about the diamonds? Zulu's empire?" she asked.

"This is a young man's game. You stay in it too long, and you end up like Zulu did. No one can avoid fate forever. Let's go away . . . tonight. Meet me at the bluffs," he said.

It didn't take much convincing. She was up and day-dreaming about sailing off into the sunset together. Finally, she would be able to love who she wanted, live how she desired, and leave all of the bullshit behind. She had so much money as a widow that they would never have to worry, and Dahlia would never be able to track them down.

By the time Dahlia realized that they had fled, they would be long gone. She dressed quickly, grabbed the keys, and raced out the door.

The bluffs. A beautiful cliff carved out of the countryside, lining the tumultuous ocean water beneath it. It was the first place that she and Ali had made love. Surrounded by nothingness, it had been far enough from Zulu's watchful eye. It was the first place Ali had brought her to make love. She remembered it as if it had happened just yesterday. He had laid her down on the blanket he had brought to cover the dirt. The sky had been so bright that it looked as if the world's most expensive chandelier twinkled above their heads. She could still smell the fresh salt from the ocean as the waves crashed into the rocks below. It was their place, far away from everyone. She was sure that no one else even knew it was there.

She navigated through the pitch-black countryside with nothing but her own headlights illuminating her path. Finally, she pulled up. Her lights shone ahead, and she saw him standing at the edge of the cliff, dressed in white linen. She threw the car into park and opened the door, placing one foot on the ground as she leaned her arm over the door. "Ali!" she called to him. The wind carried her voice to his ears, and he turned toward her.

He extended his hand, and she left the car, leaving the door open and the lights shining as she approached him. When their fingertips met, she smiled, but it dissipated when she saw the troubled look on his face. His expression was almost pained. He pulled her to his body and hugged her tightly, squeezing her body as he grasped her long, kinky, natural mane.

"I'm sorry," he whispered.

She pulled back and frowned. "What?"

She heard the hum of vehicles, and she turned toward the sound of car doors slamming. She peered curiously, but couldn't see past the shining of her own headlights.

"Who is that?" she asked frantically. She looked at him desperately for answers, still clinging to him. "Ali?"

She saw the silhouettes of men and a curvaceous outline that could only belong to one woman.

"What did you do?" she asked, heartbroken.

The woman walked in their direction until Dahlia's face finally came into view. She wore white editor's pants with an animal-print button-up Versace blouse. She looked more ready to shoot a fashion spread than to commit the acts she had planned.

"Harrah, darling, you disappoint me," Dahlia said. "Women like you are so sickening. I gave you a chance to save yourself, and you chose to save a man. You see how it ended up when I put the same choice in his hands. Men are selfish; that's why they are the rulers of the world. As soon as you told him that I wanted him dead, Ali came to find me. He told me of your betrayal and cut a deal for himself."

Harrah let go of Ali as if she had suddenly been burned by fire. The deceit was too much to handle. She had been duped by the person for whom she had risked it all.

SLAP!

Her hand whipped across his face so quickly that he never saw it coming. "How could you? How could you? You bastard!" she screamed as she cried and beat his chest.

Sadness filled his gaze. "I'm sorry."

He clasped her wrists to stop her assault, but she snatched her hands away. "Don't touch me!"

She backpedaled, moving around Dahlia as she turned to run, but there was no escaping this dreadful night. She ran right into the men of the African Mafia. She felt like a stray dog that had been cornered in an alley as she ran back and forth, trying to decide where to go.

"You see, Harrah, Ali came to me after you warned him of my threats. He offered me a partnership. He knows the business, he can put in the work, and he and I have reached a mutual and equally beneficial understanding. There was one stipulation to our treaty, however. I told him to lure you here. Since you betrayed me, all bets are off between you and me."

"Please," Harrah begged. She shook her head from side to side as she watched Salim step up. "Salim! You cannot let her do this."

Dahlia chuckled softly. "Don't beg. It doesn't become you."

Salim opened his arms, and Harrah fell into them. He felt a sense of responsibility toward her. They had come to know each other well over the years. This would be one death that would forever weigh on his conscience. "Shh, don't cry. I will make sure that it is quick. No pain. Soon you will soar in the sky with the rest of the angels. Look up . . ."

She trembled as she looked back at Ali.

"Don't look at him," Salim said. "Look up into the sky. I want the last thing you see to be true beauty, Harrah."

Harrah lifted her eyes to the sky as she sobbed and tears fell down her face.

BOOM!

In one swift movement, Salim placed a gun beneath her chin and fired a bullet up and directly into her brain. She immediately became dead weight in his arms. Salim grinned to Ali before stepping back among the goons behind him.

Dahlia turned to Ali, whose eyes had misted as he stared at the burgundy blood trail that was seeping into the dirt.

"Don't cry. You will be joining her shortly," she said.

She turned to walk away, and Ali's face fell in confusion, in anger. "We had a deal!"

"I don't make deals with disloyal mu'fuckas. If you did this to the woman you loved, imagine what you would do to me," Dahlia said knowingly.

"You bitch! Don't you walk away from me! You whore! Don't you fucking turn your back on me!" Ali's voice boomed in the night, but Dahlia ignored him. As she walked toward her waiting vehicle, a group of her goons walked toward Ali. Her driver opened the door for her. She stepped one foot inside while leaving the other on the gravel below.

"Wait," she said, staring straight ahead.

Ali's screams erupted, and Dahlia smirked in satisfaction, knowing that her bidding was being done. She lifted her second foot into the car.

She rolled down her window to address Salim. "Make sure they bring me a trophy. The five families will want proof."

ELEVEN

EVERYTHING SEEMED TO MOVE IN SLOW MOTION as Dahlia stood behind Salim. The heads of the five families represented the most powerful criminal entities in all of Africa. Not the typical gangsters. They were elderly and feeble, and their appearance would make you underestimate them, but Dahlia had heard many street tales about the moves that they had made. Their syndicates had put in work all over the world, and their reputations preceded them. The quickened rhythm of her pulse thundered in her ears. She was nervous. In the presence of greatness, she realized that everything was on the line. This was the moment she had been waiting for.

"Salim, what are you doing here, and with a guest at that? You know the rules. I find your intrusion disrespectful," one of the men said. He sat with his hands folded neatly on the table, and he peered at Salim through his one good eye. He bore a scar on the left side of his face, a long, deep gash that went right over his eye, causing it to droop low. Dahlia wondered silently how he had gotten such a scar, and the thought of the fate of the one who had put it there sent chills down her spine.

"I mean no disrespect, dear elder," Salim said, hands steepled in front of his body as if he were about to pray. "I assure you this intrusion will be to the liking of all of you."

"She is a woman. Women do not belong at this table," the elder said sternly in disapproval.

"I will make it worth your while." Dahlia spoke up as she took a step forward. She was tired of the old-school politicking. Yes, she was a woman, but she was also a boss and didn't need any man taking a stand for her. "I can speak for myself."

The old man waved his hand and sat back in his seat with a loud exhale, as if she were wasting his time. "You have two minutes."

Dahlia wasted no time cutting to the chase. "I want Zulu's seat," she said.

"Zulu's seat is reserved. Now, if you have no other matters, you can see yourself out."

Dahlia's eyebrows rose at the blatant disregard for her request, and she had to close her mouth to stop her slick tongue from responding with sharp wit. These men were old-fashioned in their ways. They thought her place was in the kitchen, not on the front lines. She was supposed to cook and clean, but Dahlia was more the hustle-and-murder type. Her mind was too brilliant to play wifey. She wanted to rule the world. In fact, if they let her in, she would eventually take one of their spots. It was just the Dahlia way. She conquered everything around her.

"I assure you that the position I wish to fill is vacant," she replied.

"Ali Akban will pick up where Zulu left off," the man replied sternly.

"Ali Akban is dead," she snapped back.

She knew that she had hit them with the unexpected when she saw the men look at one another in uncertainty.

"You don't believe me?" she asked.

Dahlia nodded, and Salim exited the room. He returned with a wool bag and passed it to Dahlia. She reached inside and placed her trophy on the table in front of the elders. Stifled gasps of horror rang out at the sight of Ali Akban's severed heard. It was wrapped in plastic, but there was no doubting that it was him.

"Ali Akban is dead. Zulu is dead. Both killed at my hand. Any other person you endorse over me will meet a similar fate. I have proved well enough that I can handle this position. All I need is your official endorsement," she said confidently, with flair and arrogance.

"Get it off of the table," the same man said, unable to tear his eyes away from the gruesome remains. He seemed to be the spokesman for the group. Salim stepped forward and placed the head back inside the bag. The man looked begrudgingly at Dahlia. He didn't want to give her anything, but he had to admit that her ruthlessness was impressive. Where fear of repercussion had halted any man from attacking Zulu or Ali, Dahlia had done it without worry. "You are either incredibly stupid or incredibly smart. I cannot tell just yet." He looked around the round table, and his peers nodded one by one. Finally, he also did so. "You have our blessing."

It took everything in Dahlia to contain her smile. Now she was official. She had the entire African Mafia behind her. It was time to take over the States one region at a time, starting with the City of Angels. It was time to get back to L.A. Her payback to Liberty and Po had not been forgotten, either, but she would put it on the back burner while she took over the game. Finally, she would be able to rule on her own. She was the king, and no one was going to knock her off the throne. Dahlia had manipulated her way to the top, and the game would never be the same.

TWELVE

CLICK. CLICK. CLICK.

The sound of Valentino stilettos stabbing the concrete echoed in the dark alley as Dahlia paced back and forth before the group of young thugs. The yellow light from the street lamp shone down upon them, and her hostages stood shivering from the lack of clothing. Her goons held them in place with pistols aimed, ready to fire at her command.

"Gentlemen," she said as she stopped walking and turned to stand squarely. "This is what you call a takeover. You've been hustling on the streets tax-free for too long. Now there are only two options. One, you hustle my product, or two, you pay rent to occupy my blocks. Any opposition will be eliminated."

She began to pace once more, her hands folded prissily in front of her, purely ladylike. "I don't expect all of you to take me seriously. I'm a woman, you think that whoever

you are working for now can protect you, you underestimate my power. I represent the African Mafia. I assure you,
there is not a gang in L.A. who can outgun me or whose
reach goes farther. It would be in your best interest to com-
ply, but should you choose not too . . ."

Her tone was flat, but her heart raced inside her chest.
This was her introduction to the Los Angeles underworld.
She was used to manipulation, but tonight she was crossing the threshold into the territory of queen pin. She was
slowly becoming a cold-blooded killer and understood that
in order to be respected, she had to instill fear. The only
thing that instilled fear was the threat of death. The streets
had to know that she was capable of pulling the trigger if
anyone stepped on her toes. She had come too far to let her
nerves get the best of her. There was no time to second-
guess her methods. She had to be willing to murder, had
to be willing to silence her conscience. The knots that filled
her stomach made it feel as if she would vomit as she was
plagued with apprehension. Yes, she had killed before, but
it was always for a reason. Someone who had crossed her
deserved to get their lights snuffed out, but none of these
men before her had done anything of the sort. She wasn't
the devil. She still had principles, but the task at hand was
completely necessary in order for her to win. It was a blood
sacrifice that must be made.

Dahlia pulled out a handgun and stepped up to one of
the hustlers.

BOOM!

Without hesitation and without flinching, she put a

bullet square between his eyes. She then stepped down the line and—*BOOM!*—she delivered another shot to a second thug. Dahlia stepped down the line, knocking off hustlers as if she were shooting ducks on the old-school Nintendo game. She turned off the guilt button of her humanity and popped them one by one. She stopped when she got to the last young man standing. He stood in the nude, trembling as he clutched his hands over his privates. He squeezed his eyes closed when it was his turn to die. He was younger than the rest yet had more courage than they did. He didn't snivel or beg as the others had done. Instead, he stood in front of her, unseeing but his chest broad and accepting of his fate.

Dahlia lowered her gun. "Open your eyes. You're going to live today," she said. She passed her pistol to Salim and stepped back.

He opened his eyes.

"Who do you work for?" she asked.

The kid remained silent, loyal to his team as he refused to answer her question.

Dahlia smirked. "Listen, you choose either to live or to die. In this moment, it is your choice. Now, answer my question. *Who* do you work for?" she repeated.

"East Side Crips," he admitted.

"Don't give me some broad answer. Give me a name," Dahlia urged.

"Mikel," he said.

"Good boy," she said. "You are my messenger. You tell Mikel that he needs to contact me within twenty-four hours, or I'm going to make every block in this neighborhood bleed."

The boy was so afraid to move that he just stood there, covering himself and shaking uncontrollably, looking straight ahead. He didn't want to look her in the eye; he was too intimidated. Darkness seemed to surround her. It was as if he was in the presence of the devil. He could feel the evil emanating from her.

"Go," her voice boomed. "Before I change my mind."

The boy took off running down the abandoned alley. Dahlia looked back at the men she had murdered in cold blood.

"Cleanup crew?" Salim asked.

Dahlia shook her head. "No, I want these murders to be known. I want my presence to be seen, felt, and heard."

"He didn't take my first threat seriously. Let's send him a message he won't soon forget," Dahlia said. It had been three days, and she had heard no word from Mikel. She had laid down six of his workers, and it irritated her to no end that she had received no reaction. If she were a man, she would be engaged in war right now. The fact that Mikel had swept their beef under the rug had Dahlia seeing red. At this very moment, she sat in the car outside Mikel's most profitable stash house while she had members of the African Mafia placed at Mikel's other trap spots across L.A. If he didn't care about his workers, she was about to target the one thing that any man loved most: his money. Dahlia had reached out to Trixie's old working girls and had a girl at each trap house waiting to create a distraction. As Dahlia watched the rear of the voluptuous prostitute ascend the steps to the house, she salivated over the victory that was near.

The hooker knocked on the door, pretending to be a customer, but the width of her hips instantly threw the dope boy who answered off of his square. With a goon posted on either side of the door, guns loaded, ready for action, they quickly spun and walked the hustler back into the house. Dahlia exited the car and walked up the stairs with three additional goons behind her for protection. She palmed a gun in her right hand, carrying it discreetly at her side as she entered the house. The dope boy had already been snuffed out and lay with a leaking hole to the forehead.

"Get the money, kill the workers," she ordered.

The three men behind her dispersed throughout the house. Their pistols were silenced, so the men working inside had no idea that Dahlia's crew was knocking them off one by one. Finally, she reached the top floor, where her men had cornered one of Mikel's workers as he kneeled in front of the safe. She entered the room, her Fendi heels announcing her presence.

"You might as well kill me, home girl, cuz I ain't saying shit." The kid was cocky as he was forced onto his knees, hands raised behind his head, baggy Dickies sagging from his behind.

Dahlia didn't have time to play. Her patience was non-existent. She wanted to speak to Mikel, and she would cause as much chaos as possible to smoke him out of his hole.

She put a heel in the kid's back, forcing him to fall forward, his hands bracing on the floor to break his fall. She immediately put her gun to one of his hands.

BOOM!

She blew a nickel-sized hole through his hand.

"Aghh! You crazy bitch!" he shouted in agony as he gripped his wrist and writhed, looking at his hand in disbelief. He rocked back and forth as he bit his lower lip. "Fuck!"

"Open the safe," she said calmly.

All of his tough-guy bravado went out the window. "OK . . . OK," he conceded. "Damn, look at my fucking hand, man!" Blood flowed everywhere as he held it up.

"Open it," she ordered. She nudged him with her gun while her men stood around.

As soon as the kid opened the safe, Dahlia put a bullet in the back of his head. He slumped forward, his head landing on the contents of the safe. She pulled his body off and smiled when she saw the piles of money that were stacked inside. There was at least a quarter million in front of her. She grabbed two thickly knotted piles of bills and made her way to the window. She lifted the pane.

"What are you doing?" Salim asked.

"This isn't a robbery. I'm just proving a point. We don't need this money. That's little paper to us. We're making it rain over the neighborhood. Giving away Mikel's hardearned money. I'm making him come to me," Dahlia said with a smirk. She tossed the money out of the window and watched as it fell slowly to the ground below.

"Merry Christmas, muthafuckas!" she shouted. She went back and forth to the safe until it was empty, causing a frenzy in the hood as people began to scramble for the free money. She walked out of the house unnoticed, her goons following her. The money was too much of a distraction for anyone to even care. She got into the car and drove away, knowing that she had just insulted Mikel's entire operation. The clash between the two of them was now inevitable.

THIRTEEN

MONEY. POWER. THE AMERICAN DREAM. DAHLIA HAD it all, and after her little stunt, she had the devotion of the entire city. Her name was being spoken on the blocks of every hood in L.A. She was not to be fucked with, she had made that crystal-clear, and now the money was flowing. Either you were paying weekly tithes to the African Mafia for their protection, or you were hustling Dahlia's products. There was no negotiating, and since she had brought conflict to Mikel's doorstep, she had not heard of even one of his traps reopening. Now that she had a hold of the lowest level of her business, she felt that it was time to tame another aspect: diamonds. While the streets were the least lucrative venture, she knew that it was important for her to turn her name into legend. As long as she had the streets, then her other business would work flawlessly. Her reputation could only be built up in the hood, on the block, and on the tips of the tongues of the people. Now that she had done that, she could elevate.

She looked around the home that the five families had purchased for her. It was her welcome gift. She was in a new league, and she appreciated the fact that she was being accepted with open arms. It was a four-bedroom beauty that sat in the Hollywood Hills. She admired the lights of the city as L.A. came to life beneath her. The space around her was empty. Much like her personal life, her home was lonely, neglected, and dark. Her thoughts momentarily drifted to Po—not of the love she had for him, because there had been none. He was a means to an end. However, when she thought of him, she thought of the love that he and Liberty had, the same love that she had ruined. He had been at the top, in the exact same place that Dahlia now occupied, only he had chosen someone to share it with. Dahlia's realm was lonely. There was no room for anyone else. She was too in love with power and control to ever share everything she had earned with another. "Fuck love, I'm married to the money," she whispered.

DING DONG!

The ringing of the doorbell announced a visitor. She knew that it could only be one person. Salim was the only other person who knew where she lived. Dahlia crossed the room and made her way to the front door. She opened it to find a large cardboard box on her doorstep. She walked outside and down the driveway until she reached the street. Her head swiveled right, then left, only to find the road deserted. Her eyes lowered into suspicious slits as she looked back at the box. Chills went down her spine. She immediately pulled out her cell phone to call Salim. She paced back and forth, feeling as if something was awry.

RING! RING!

Dahlia's head snapped toward the box as the sound of a ringing cell phone blared through the air. Her stomach knotted, and she walked slowly back toward her front door. She lifted the flap on the box.

Blood. Salim. Chopped into pieces and wrapped in clear plastic. His dead eyes were wide open as he stared up at her, hauntingly. She backpedaled, tripping over her own feet, as fear and shock pushed her against the door frame. Vomit tickled the back of her throat, and she couldn't stop herself from keeling over. She gripped the side of her house as she lost her composure on the manicured lawn.

She reached down and picked up the white letter that was taped to the box: "Beverly Wilshire Hotel. 9:00 P.M."

Dahlia balled up the note and exhaled sharply as she put a fist to her forehead in distress. Anger pulsed through her, and she bit her bottom lip. She knew exactly who was behind this. She had been struck, but it was a low blow. Her counsel had been taken from her. Salim was like a crutch to her. He made her transition into power much easier, because his wisdom guided her choices. Now that he was gone, the weight that he had carried seemed to build on her shoulders.

Although she had committed some deplorable acts in the past, the unexpected sight of Salim's remains disturbed her. She knew that she couldn't reach out to her men to dispose of the body. She trusted no one enough to let them know where she rested her head. Frustrated and pressed for time, she knew that she would have to move the body herself. Leaving it out in the open would raise suspicions. She stepped out of her Louboutins and pushed the box off of her porch. It took all of her strength to get the box to her garage. Sweat had formed on her forehead, and she heaved as she tried to calm herself. A calm mind made rationale decisions. The last thing she wanted to do was panic.

She rushed back to retrieve her shoes and then swiftly got into her car and backed it out of the garage. She ensured that the garage closed behind her before pulling off into the night.

Goose bumps formed on her arms as she sat in front of the five-star hotel. She checked the clip of the small .22 handgun that she kept tucked beneath her car seat. It was full, and although it wasn't heavy, it would keep a nigga up off of her if she found herself in a bind. She exited the car. It was the first time she had been without protection since becoming affiliated with the African mob. She felt naked without her goons there ready to buck at the inkling of trouble. It was just her against an unknown enemy. Mikel may as well have been a ghost. She only had a name. Dahlia had no idea what he looked like, but tonight he had shown her what he was capable of. She had underestimated his gangster. Salim had been the price to pay. She had to be careful and move smart.

As she looked at the hotel, her nerves settled slightly. *He's not going to do anything in a public place. He picked this spot so that it could remain civil, at least for now,* she thought. She checked her rearview mirror before she got out of the car. She discreetly tucked the pistol into her Birkin and then swiftly trotted across the street. Her long, toned legs were complemented by the red-soled heels that graced her feet. She wore a trench coat and a silk scarf draped in true Hollywood fashion around her face. She looked like a posh heiress, which helped her blend in perfectly with the night scene of the rich and famous who frequented Rodeo Drive. She entered the hotel, every single one of her senses on full alert. The smell of fresh-cut flowers met her nose instantly. The sound of mixed chatter flooded her ears. Goose bumps formed on her neck from the cold air that circulated throughout the building. Most important, her eyes were all-seeing as her neck swiveled from left to right.

Dahlia was on edge. She didn't like the fact that her enemy had her at a disadvantage. Mikel knew exactly what she looked like, whereas she may as well have been blind. Any one of the men in the room could have been Mikel, and there was no way for her to distinguish friend from foe.

Dahlia turned on her heels, scanning the lobby, and then decided to wait at the chic lounge. She would rather blend in with the crowd than stand in the lobby out in the open, looking like an easy mark. She sat on one of the stools in the crowded bar and turned around so that her back leaned against the countertop and her eyes were on the door. Impatience turned to anger as she sat, checking her watch every few minutes. A tap on the bar caused her to turn to find a striking redheaded bartender sliding her a drink and giving her a friendly smile.

"Here you go," the bartender said.

"I didn't order this," Dahlia responded.

The bartender pointed to a table in the corner of the room. "The gentleman over there put you on his open tab and sent it over," the girl responded.

Dahlia's eyes shot to the corner of the room. "Mikel," she whispered.

"Let me know if there is anything else that I can get you," the girl said.

Dahlia dismissed her with a wave of her hand and then focused on Mikel. He was everything other than what she had expected. She had thought she would be meeting with some hoodlum, a gang leader with a body count that was reflected in tattoo art on his face. She had expected baggy pants and gangster swag, but the man she saw was so inconspicuous and well put together that she was thrown off guard. He looked more like a Fortune 500 Wall Street guy than the head of a criminal enterprise.

He was strikingly handsome, with Spanish features. His dark hair was slicked back neatly. The Ferragamo suit he wore was custom-tailored into a slim fit, hugging his athletic build nicely. He was mysterious and at the same time one of the most attractive men she had ever laid eyes on. How had she missed him when she had scanned the bar?

He lifted his glass to her with a smirk of amusement on his face. Clearly, he had been watching her as she watched out for him. Just as she suspected, he had the upper hand. She stood and crossed the room, her body's curves gaining her unwanted attention. She turned down numerous pursuits before she finally landed before his table.

"I take it you would be Mikel?" she asked.

The man shook his head and then nodded behind her. "That is Mikel," he said. Dahlia turned around as she suddenly felt cornered. Her eyes scanned the room. "He's the Mexican kid, white button-up, jeans, by the bar." Dahlia spotted him and simultaneously noticed the slight bulge on his hip where his pistol rested. She turned back to the man in front of her. "I am Jacob Mares. I'm his connect," he said.

Dahlia smirked, knowing that no matter where he was getting his dope from, she was much more major. It didn't matter if he was from Cuba, Colombia, the Dominican Republic, or wherever. There was no cocaine, no heroin, no diamonds comparable to those found in Africa.

"The money that you poured into the streets belonged to me."

"You don't own those streets. I do. And unless you pay me, you're not going to occupy them long," she replied smoothly.

Jacob smiled charmingly, sat back, and crossed one leg over the other. It was such a feminine move, but when he did it, Dahlia thought nothing of the sort. He owned her attention as his arm draped casually across the back of the booth. "You are a unique woman," he said.

"I'm a woman who means what she says."

"I didn't call you here to engage in a war of wit," Jacob answered. "I know who you are. I've done my research. The entity that you represent is very powerful. I would like to propose somewhat of a partnership."

Dahlia laughed.

Jacob stood and walked behind her, purposefully rubbing his crotch against her behind as he reached around her body to pull out her chair. "Please sit. Hear me out," he offered. "Please just hear me out."

Dahlia obliged reluctantly and watched him like a hawk as he rounded the table to reclaim his seat. "I don't need a partner," she said.

"I've been doing business in these streets for years, love. I know the ins, the outs. I know the major players. I know the heads of all the gangs. I also know that drugs are minuscule on your scale. I know your ties with the Africans. You deal diamonds, not dope. You have access to women and jewels. You don't have time to focus on the street element. I could introduce you to some very important men, men who buy the type of product to which you have access."

"I know men who buy diamonds. I don't need you," Dahlia said smugly as she sipped her drink.

"You don't know men who buy women, though, or women who buy women, for that matter. There is an entire network of wealthy businessmen who will pay to play," Jacob stated. "You have no idea the amount of money you are missing."

Now he had her attention. The main reason Dahlia had focused on the dope game first was that she was familiar with it. Selling sex was much harder. She had to establish the right circle in order to step into human trafficking. She didn't know if she was ready. The thought of that realm was highly intimidating.

"So you would extend this network to me, but what do you get in return? Full run of *my* streets?" Dahlia asked.

"Yes, but the trade-off will be worth it. I won't pay you to move product on those blocks, but I can purchase my product from you for a good price," he stated.

"You want me to become your connect," she concluded.

"You say connect, I say partner. It is a win-win," Jacob said. "Neither of us wants to enter into a war. It will attract attention. It will put the spotlight on, and neither you nor I will make money from it."

"You have already smacked my cheek," Dahlia replied as she peered at him. "You kill my right hand and send him to me in a box, but you talk as if you don't want war. That is war."

Dahlia noticed the color drain from Jacob's face, and she turned around to see what had caused him such a fright. She was shocked when she saw her own men, members of the African Mafia—her protection—entering the bar. She hadn't even requested their presence. She had told no one where she was going, but somehow they knew when she needed their protection. She was apparently never left alone or unprotected. There was always someone watching. She hadn't ordered them to stand down, so she was guarded at all times. She watched as her goons positioned themselves discreetly around the room.

"As you can see, we did not appreciate the loss of one of our own," Dahlia said smoothly. She had no idea how her men knew where she was, but at that moment, she was more than grateful for their presence.

Jacob had lost his leverage in the conversation. "I do not want war with the African mob, but I will engage in it if it comes to that. Let's avoid that and go into business together. We stand to make more money together than we could ever make apart. I only want the streets; the rest is yours. I can get you in the door and introduce you to the people who can take you to the next level. Let me have the drugs. Human trafficking is your game."

Dahlia knew that she could easily get connected through the five families, but she didn't want to go to them for assistance. She was still proving herself to them. If she couldn't bring new money to the table, they would not respect her. She needed to show that her entity was self-sufficient. She was still earning her respect with the five families. She had been initiated begrudgingly. If she could show that she had her own connections, it would make their acceptance of her much easier. She watched Jacob watching her as she sat thinking in silence. The unlikely partnership could prove quite profitable, but she was still unsure. Her trust was not easily earned.

"How do you suppose we put our current beefs to rest? I lined up your men, shot them down in the streets like dogs. That is not exactly the type of foundation I like to start a partnership on," she said.

"A small price to pay for a step toward greatness," Jacob responded.

Dahlia nodded and raised her glass. "Agreed," she said. She sipped her champagne, and Jacob did the same, sealing their new deal.

He stood and pulled a knot of money out of his pocket. He placed the entire thing on the table.

"What exactly is that for?" she asked.

"For your attire. You are my date for the Gentlemen's Ball," he replied.

"Date? I'm not interested in dating you, Jacob. This is business, and I don't need your money," she answered, and flicked the wad with her long red fingernails, causing the hundred-dollar bills to spread out across the table.

"Being on my arm is the only way you will get it, toots. Don't flatter yourself," Jacob responded with a slick smile. "The Gentleman's Ball is where you will find your most loyal customers. They are in the market to purchase women. I'm pulling you into an elite circle. So take the money. It's a black-tie affair. I'll send a driver to pick you up Friday night." He rounded the table and stopped when he was near her side. He bent down to whisper in her ear. "And if I wanted to taste you, I wouldn't have to pay for it. You'd give it to me again and again and again." His lips touched her ear as he spoke, and the scent of his cologne intoxicated her. She gasped as sparks of electricity caused her clitoris to swell. "See you Friday," Jacob finished, before walking out of the bar, suavely buttoning his suit jacket as he departed.

Dahlia licked her lips and shook her head as she finished her drink. She would have to be careful with Jacob. His charm was distracting. Little did Jacob know, she wasn't looking for a partner. Once she acquired his connections, she would kill him. She didn't share her throne under any circumstances.

FOURTEEN

PO AND ROCKO SAT IN THE SUITE of the MGM Grand, overlooking the city of Detroit. Po stared out the window while Rocko cleaned his gun on the bed. The strain on their friendship was evident, but both men couldn't deny that they had love for each other. They had come up together and genuinely didn't want to see any harm come to each other. They were both preoccupied by their own thoughts. Rocko hadn't been able to take his mind off of Liberty, and to keep himself from acting on his true feelings, he steered clear of her. Po, on the other hand, wasn't concerned about Liberty at all. He couldn't shake thoughts of Dahlia. Although he knew she was bad news, there was something about her that kept him wanting her. Maybe it was the mind-blowing sex. Or maybe it was her smooth cocoa skin and slight accent. Whatever it was, he wanted more. His thoughts were clouded, and he needed to feel what Dahlia provided for him. She had a way of making him feel powerful. His thoughts were interrupted by Rocko's comment.

"So you say the ol'-school nigga is connected, huh?" Rocko said, referring to Baron.

"Yeah, basically, he ran a black Cosa Nostra. Baron is a legend in the city," Po answered, still focusing on the city's skyline.

"So you mean to tell me Liberty was connected to this nigga all the time and never plugged us? He needs to see what's up on a new coke connect. If you say he has it, what are we waiting for? Let's step to the man," Rocko said, getting straight to the point. They were in a new city with no connections, so Rocko was definitely thinking about his next move. He wasn't a nine-to-five type of guy, so the only thing he knew was to hustle.

"You know what? That isn't a bad idea. You looking at the nigga all crazy didn't help us any," Po said sarcastically. What Rocko said had struck a chord with Po; if he could get on through Baron, he would easily take over the city of Detroit. He needed a come-up, and Baron was his way in. He told himself that he would immediately begin to work on that connection. He went over and grabbed his cell phone and called Liberty, putting her up on the grand scheme. After a half hour of persuading her to set their future up by plugging them, she agreed. She told Po that Baron was asleep and she would mention it to him the following day. When Po hung up the phone, he rubbed his hands together and imagined himself taking over Detroit.

* * *

The sun's beams woke up Baron as he lay on the couch of Liberty's home. He had been in Mexico for so long hiding it felt funny not waking up to humid weather and the call of the rooster. He slowly sat up and stretched his arms out. The smell of bacon and eggs crept into his nose, and he looked behind him to see Liberty cooking. She was fully dressed and obviously had been up for a while. After their long conversation the night before, he had asked her if he could stay the night. He didn't have a lot of money and didn't want to take the risk of being caught on camera at any of the hotels. His face was infamous in Detroit, and he wanted to stay as low-key as possible.

"Smells good," he said as he stood up and wiped the cold out of his eyes.

"Good morning! Thank you." Liberty placed the plates on the table.

Baron joined her. The only thing he was looking for was clarity, and he got that. He had no reason to stay in the States and run the risk of the feds picking him up. He had a life sentence waiting for him, and he wasn't trying to do a day.

"I'm going to head out later this evening. I wish I could help you out monetarily, but things aren't like they used to be," Baron said almost shamefully. He had been living modestly and low-key, not spending above his means. His secret overseas accounts were keeping him afloat.

"It's fine. I don't need any money. I am going to find a job and move back here permanently," Liberty said.

She had never had a job in her life, and she was looking forward to getting out in the real world. However, the conversation she had with Po earlier that morning kept playing in her head. He had suggested that she ask Baron to plug him and Rocko with a coke connect. She had been battling about asking him all morning; she just didn't know how.

"I have something to ask you," Liberty said just before she slid a forkful of eggs into her mouth.

"What's on your mind?" Baron asked as he proceeded to eat his food.

"Well, as you know, Po and Rocko have been watching my back since A'shai died. I just wanted to make sure they were good, so I'm asking for your help," Liberty said, obviously beating around the bush.

"Continue," Baron said calmly, wanting to hear what she had in mind.

"Obviously, they know who you are. Everyone in Detroit knows who you are. They were wondering if you could introduce them to a couple of your friends, ya know, plug them?" Liberty asked nervously, not knowing what type of response she would get.

Baron stopped eating and put his fork down. He slowly sat back in his chair and folded his arms across his chest. He looked into Liberty's eyes, trying to see if she was serious. He didn't expect that coming from her. His first notion was to say no, but as a calculated thinking man, he paused and gave it a long thought.

"To be honest with you, Liberty . . . my first thought

was to say no. I do not know these two guys you speak of. A strong coke connect is something that comes with hard work, hustle, and longevity. However, I want nothing but the best for you. So I'm going to give you some game, and I want you to listen close."

Baron moved the plate from in front of him. He then placed his clasped hands on the table. He took a deep breath and had already laid out a plan in his head, just that quick. Being at the height of drug dealing, Baron had learned to sort thoughts out in his head quickly, which was a trait of a great leader.

"I'm going to introduce you to a couple of plugs. This way, they will always need you. You will be the link to them and the money. As you get older, you will understand that people and circumstances change. You can't trust people . . . trust greed. Their greed will keep them loyal to you," Baron said, trying to break it down for Liberty in its simplest form.

Liberty listened closely, and it all started to make sense to her. Baron was introducing her to another angle. By no means was she built for the game, but what he said was advice she could use for everyday life.

"You understand?" Baron asked. He could see that she was thinking about what he had said. It was as if he opened a hallway in her mind that she never knew about.

"I understand," she answered.

"Good. There is something called the Gentlemen's Ball in . . ." Baron started. He stopped in mid-sentence, remembering that Liberty was very familiar with that ball. It was the same ball at which she had reunited with A'shai years back.

"I know what the ball is," she whispered as her thoughts drifted to her haunting past.

He continued after a brief pause. "Well, I want to take you there, and I have powerful friends I can connect with while there. I have been out of the loop for years, but this will get me back into my old practice."

"I don't know about going there," Liberty said as she thought about that particular time in her life when she was auctioned off. She didn't want to relive the pain that had scarred her for life. The last time she was there, she was half naked on a stage as if she was a piece of meat rather than a human being. Her face was filled with pain and sorrow. She closed her eyes and shook her head as she tried to get the images out of her mind.

"Listen." Baron said as he placed his hand on Liberty's. "The only way to conquer your fears is to face them. I know you have bad memories there, but to revisit the same place as a stronger woman will free you. You are a different woman, and this is the last step to letting all of the pain go."

Liberty smiled. Baron was so comforting, and she instantly saw where A'shai had gotten his strength and charm. "OK. I trust you. Let's do it," Liberty said. It was set. She was about to get connected. She thought about what Baron had said to her about keeping Po and Rocko dependent on her, so that they would always need her. She decided to be the middle man rather than just plugging Po in directly. The way he handled the Dahlia situation had her on the ropes about him. She didn't trust Po the way she once had. It was perfect timing, because the ball was a couple of weeks away.

Baron promised himself he would establish the connection and disappear again . . . like a ghost.

FIFTEEN

IT WAS THE NIGHT OF THE GENTLEMEN'S Ball, the one night of the year when the underworld's elite met. That particular event served more than one purpose for its patrons. It was a night when the richest criminals in the world had a chance to buy sexual favors, but it also was a top-shelf networking mixer. It was a night when many men made connections and illegal business arrangements that lasted for years. It was a special night for the real gangsters. Baron and his date, Liberty, had just flown in and were definitely going to be in the building. Baron kept his word, and before he returned to Tijuana, he would establish connections for Liberty and her friends.

The event was exclusive and by invitation only. Each year, a five-star hotel was rented out for the gathering. No cameras or phones were allowed inside the building. Politicians and tycoons also were in attendance. The allure of sexual slaves from different parts of the world was too much for the men to resist. The night's air was perfect as the full moon sat in the sky. The stage was set to be magical.

Liberty had butterflies in her stomach as she held the arm of Baron. The last time she had been at the exquisite hotel, she was on the menu as a call girl. Now she was on the arm of one of the biggest gangsters in the world. She had come full circle. As they stepped out of the limo, Baron held his arm out for Liberty and gave her a smile. He could sense that she was nervous, so he gave her his famous smile, and it seemed as if her worries melted away.

Baron looked like his old self. He had cut his beard into a neat goatee, and his head was clean-shaven. His Italian-cut suit fit him to perfection, and he felt like himself again. Baron hadn't been to the ball in years, and he had done enough favors to get fronted whatever he wanted. The world was his, and he was glad to be back in the limelight.

As they walked into the entrance, an old business colleague walked in with them.

"Baron Montgomery," Anari said as she extended her manicured hand. She was a fair-skinned African American lady in her early forties. Baron hadn't seen Anari in years and was happy to see an old friend. He extended his hand and shook hers, followed by a quick peck on her check. He then focused on her husband, Von, who was also in "the industry."

"Von. Anari. How are you guys?" he asked the power couple.

"We're good. I hear you're a wanted man," Von said jokingly, knowing that Baron had made *America's Most Wanted*.

They all shared a laugh, and Baron fixed his tie as if boasting that he hadn't been caught. "They can't catch what they can't see," he replied with a charming smile.

Anari turned her attention to Liberty, who seemed out of the loop. "You have a beautiful date," she said as she focused on Liberty's beauty.

"She is beautiful, isn't she?" Baron said as he looked at Liberty and winked his eye. This brought a smile to Liberty's face. "This is my daughter, Liberty." Baron put his arm around Liberty and kissed her on her forehead.

Liberty's heart warmed, and she closed her eyes and was caught in the moment. It felt so good to hear Baron say that about her. She honestly felt like his daughter, and it was the best feeling in the world to her.

"Hello, Liberty," Anari said as she and then Von held their hands out to greet her.

Liberty shook both of their hands, and there was something about them that she liked. The woman had a powerful aura about herself, and Liberty picked up on it immediately. Maybe it was because she was one of the biggest cocaine providers in the country. She had a direct plug with the Supreme Clientele table, the biggest drug syndicate in the world. That one table had connections to anything illegal and at the best price. Anari was the boss, and the boss energy beamed off of her.

"Sorry to hear about your loss a couple of years back,"

Anari said, referring to Willow, whom Baron had lost in the midst of a street beef.

Baron nodded, accepting her condolences. "Well, I guess I will see you on the inside," he said as he headed toward the door.

They parted and entered the ballroom. The place was splendid, and the sounds of smooth jazz danced through the air as the live band played for the patrons. A beautiful, heavy-set black woman skillfully zatted to the beat, giving the place a calm ambience. Her band members wore tuxedos, and they closed their eyes as they grooved to the sound of their own musical genius. A big runway sat on the main floor, and memories began to bombard Liberty's thoughts. Years ago, she walked that same runway, waiting to get picked by the highest bidder.

"Everything is going to be OK. That was the old you. This is the best way to bury those old memories. You have to confront them head-on," Baron said as he felt her shoulders tense up while having his arm around them.

"I'm OK," Liberty said as she tried to remain unmoved. "I'm OK," she repeated, this time with a slight grin, showing that she was fine.

Beautiful women walked around with masquerade masks, serving champagne from silver trays. Liberty grabbed a glass from one of the trays and quickly downed it.

"I needed that," she said, making Baron laugh.

It seemed as if the whole building heard Baron's quiet chuckle, because all eyes were on them at that point. Everyone had heard about Baron's mysterious disappearance from the law, and it only added to his legend. It made him Mr. Untouchable. He had managed to shake the feds and disappear into thin air. People flocked to him, and Baron noticed that he was about to become the center of attention. It was exactly what he wanted. He would establish a connection for Liberty, and his mission would be complete.

Baron whispered in Liberty's ear as different men began to come his way. "Let me mingle for a second. Go and find us a seat before the auction starts," he instructed. He began to extend his hand for handshakes as people started to crowd around him. Liberty nodded in compliance and headed to the main floor to find a table for them.

Dahlia's red-soled stilettos were the first thing in sight as she stepped out of the tinted SUV. She wore an all-black dress that hugged her body tightly, displaying all of her curves. Her makeup was precise, and the black lipstick she wore gave her a sinister but sexy look. Jacob accompanied her, but he was a mere accessory to the stunning Dahlia.

They entered the Gentlemen's Ball together. Dahlia had been looking forward to this once-in-a-lifetime opportunity. Although she was very wealthy and successful at what she did, her greed pushed her to accumulate more. She had an insatiable appetite, and she was ready to expand.

Dahlia put her arm inside Jacob's as he led the way onto the ballroom floor. She immediately noticed the small crowd gathering around a tall, dark, and handsome man.

"Who is that?" she whispered to Jacob, wondering who was this man causing such a ruckus.

"Well, I'll be damned. That's Baron Montgomery. I thought he was dead or something," Jacob said as he stared in admiration.

"Who is Baron Montgomery?" Dahlia asked, becoming more intrigued by the second. While asking questions, she never took her eyes off of him.

"He was a heavy supplier a couple of years back. He had the whole Midwest region locked, with deep political connections. That's until he got under fire with the feds. He went into hiding and disappeared," Jacob said, giving her a brief breakdown of what he knew about him.

Dahlia didn't know what it was about the older gentleman, but she wanted to meet him. Men who commanded respect among their peers attracted Dahlia. It literally got her wet when she saw a well-respected man who held a position of power. She loved taking a man everyone admired and breaking him down, making him submit to her. It was slowly becoming an obsession for her. Her hunger for total domination was borderline insane, and at that moment, Dahlia wanted to seduce that tall, dark man whom everyone called Baron Montgomery. Dahlia felt her kitty beginning to purr, and she began to wet her inner thighs at the thought of taking control of him. Her nipples hardened at the sight of the people hanging on his every word. She slowly took her arm from Jacob's and strutted past the crowd, making sure she shifted her weight left to right. She knew that she was blessed with a big, round ass and used it to her advantage.

Her wide hips demanded attention, and she looked back, and just as she expected, all eyes were on her. She locked eyes with Baron and made love to him through that stare, and he felt it. People say eyes can talk, and the saying was proved right at that moment. Dahlia had just told him that she wanted him bad without even opening her mouth. She ran her tongue over the top row of her teeth just before she turned her head and broke the stare-down. Dahlia headed toward the bathroom, knowing that Baron would follow. She didn't give a damn about Jacob; she had used him to get in the door, and that was all she needed. He was useless to her at that point.

Baron couldn't take his eyes off the beautiful chocolate goddess who had just fucked him with her eyes. He looked at the tight dress that hugged her hips and the way her hard nipples protruded through the dress, displaying that she wore no bra. She was one of the most beautiful, voluptuous women he had ever seen. Naturally, his eyes followed her ass as she headed toward the restrooms in the corner of the place. There was something about her that made Baron want to know more about her. He cut off his sentence midway through and excused himself from the group of men to whom he was talking. He had to see what was up with this mystery lady.

He smoothly made his way toward her as the woman looked back at him and smiled, before she disappeared into the restroom. It was as if she was daring him to follow. Baron returned the smile. It was obvious that she was giving chase.

"OK, I get it. She's playing cat and mouse," Baron said under his breath, and he calmly made his way to the restrooms. He usually wouldn't behave the way he was, but the woman had a certain mystique about herself. He had to see who she was. The curiosity was killing him. He fixed his tie and pushed open the ladies' restroom door. The sight alone made his manhood begin to grow. She was leaning against the sink with her legs and arms crossed, as if she was waiting on him.

"What's your name?" Dahlia said as she gave him a sexy half smile.

"I'm Baron Montgomery," Baron said in his low, smooth baritone.

Dahlia loved what she was seeing. His neat salt-and-pepper beard and broad shoulders were a turn-on for her. He slid his hands into his slacks and slowly walked over to her, taking his time but looking directly into her eyes.

"And what's your name?" Baron asked as he stood about a foot away from her.

Dahlia took her time as she was strategically laying her trap for the man in front of her. She rolled her eyes, unfolded her arms, and reached for his crotch. "It doesn't matter what my name is. All you need to know is that I am soaking wet and ready to feel that chocolate pole inside of me. Ooh," she said as she squirmed and closed her eyes, imagining him inside of her. She dropped her hand lower and felt his semi-erect penis.

Baron was surprised by her blatant aggressiveness. He had never seen a beautiful woman be so assertive when it came to sex. He couldn't help but get aroused by her touch. Dahlia grabbed Baron's hand and guided it under her dress and then eventually into her panties. Baron felt her wetness and was surprised by how soaked she was. He had never felt anything like it. She had hair on her love box, so it felt like a wet kitten as Baron slipped his index finger inside her, and Dahlia spread her legs a bit wider and began to pant heavily while rolling her eyes in the back of her head. She pushed out a small squirt on command as she felt an orgasm approaching. She was so horny that she couldn't control herself. She released herself all over Baron fingers and dripped onto the floor, causing a small puddle. Dahlia was pulling out all of her tricks. Her oversized clitoris was rock-hard, and she wanted the powerful stranger inside of her. Baron instantly yanked his hand back and shook his head. He knew exactly what he was doing, and that was showing her who was boss. He had too much class to have sex in a restroom, and the absence of a woman in his life over the past years had blinded him for a moment. However, he had snapped back to his truth and knew that he would never do anything of that sort in a public place, no matter how beautiful the woman. He walked to the sink and washed his hands. He headed out the door, and just before he exited, he looked back and smiled at her. Now he was the cat . . . not the mouse.

Liberty walked around the main floor and couldn't help but relive the first time she was there and remember the night she had gotten sold to Samad. She found a fancy decorated table and took a seat, and it all came back to her. She glanced at the stage and saw a familiar face peek out from behind the curtains.

"Oh, my God," Liberty said as she began to tear up. It was Abia, the madam of the Gentlemen's Ball. Abia looked older, but she still was as pretty as Liberty remembered. The crow's feet on the sides of her eyes displayed Abia's age, and she had gained a little bit of weight. However, Liberty knew that it was she. Abia had taught Liberty the art of seduction. Instantly, Liberty had a flashback to the night she was sold by Abia. It was vivid, as if it had happened the previous night. Liberty closed her eyes and thought back to the time when she prepared to walk onto the stage to auction herself to the highest bidder.

Liberty looked in the vanity mirror as she applied the mascara to her eyes. Butterflies fluttered in the pit of stomach. She prepared for the biggest night of the year. Abia stood behind her with her arms crossed, watching the beauty doll herself up.

"You look gorgeous," Abia complimented her as she placed her hands on Liberty's shoulders.

"Thank you," Liberty answered.

She had been hearing about this ball for so long and wondered what to expect when she went out to the show room. She could hear the chatter from the men and the soft music playing, and it only added to her nervousness. Liberty's hand began to tremble as she applied the eyeliner to her lids.

"Don't be afraid. You are going to do great," Abia said as

she took notice of the young damsel in distress. "It's just like any other trick, but it's for a lot more money."

Abia thought about the high-ticket price that Liberty would demand. Hands down, she was the most stunning woman in the building, and Abia understood that. Abia already knew whose attention she would get, and that was Samad Ali, one of the biggest cocaine distributors in the country. Samad always purchased the belle of the ball each year, and she knew that this year, he would be amazed. Inside Abia's head, she knew that if everything went as planned, Samad would buy Liberty, not only for the night but also for life.

At the end of the day, Liberty belonged to Abia, and she was nothing more than cattle waiting to be sold to the highest bidder, despite the illusion of friendship that Abia put on. Since the ball was held in a hotel, it acted as a gigantic brothel for the night, and soon the rooms would be filled with married men and Abia's girls engaging in various sexual acts and all different types of fetishes. Abia already began to think about how she would make a million dollars in one single night. She closed her eyes and smiled and prepared for the biggest trick of the year.

Liberty snapped back to reality and wanted to talk to Abia. Even though Abia, in hindsight, had pimped her, Liberty had a place in her heart for her. It was a weird feeling, but Abia was like a mother figure to Liberty in a strange way. Liberty stood up and headed to the door that led backstage.

SIXTEEN

"SUCK THOSE STOMACHS IN TIGHTLY, AND MAKE sure everything is tucked in," Abia said as she slowly walked down the line of girls. "I swear, I don't even know how some of you made it into the brothels," she snapped under her breath. She inspected each girl's body and makeup thoroughly, looking them all up and down carefully. The auction started in thirty minutes, and she wanted every girl to look as enticing and perfect as possible. "Beauty is pain, remember that," she reminded them as she tightened a girl's corset, pulling it as tight as she could, morphing the slim girl's body even more.

Abia planned for this day all year, and it was the only day of the year when she could clear one million dollars easy. People would be surprised if they knew how much powerful and wealthy men would pay for exotic "quiet" pussy. Abia offered a service no one else in the country could provide. Men could cheat on their wives, indulge their sexual fantasies, or simply buy women without the risk of their secret getting out. She had done this for years, and she hadn't had one case of one of her clients getting exposed. She was the best in the business, and all the upper echelon in the game understood that.

As Abia tied up the girl, her eyes drifted to the young lady who stood by the door. She squinted and looked closer. It was Liberty, her favorite girl who had ever come through her long line of girls. Abia quickly snapped her fingers, calling one of her assistants over. She stared at Liberty while talking to the assistant.

"Take over for me for a second."

Abia headed toward Liberty and put her hands over her mouth. She began to tear up as she approached.

"Is that you?" Abia said as she extended her arms for an embrace.

"Yeah, it's me," Liberty said, and she hugged Abia.

They both rocked back and forth, hugging each other as tightly as they could. It was a beautiful scene as they reunited. As they released each other, Abia grabbed both of Liberty's hands and leaned back to look at her.

"You are still beautiful. My million-dollar baby," Abia said, referring to the price that Liberty had sold for years back, which still was a record yet to be touched. Liberty didn't know it, but she was a legend in the call-girl game. Every girl heard stories about Abia's "million-dollar baby," and they aspired to do what Liberty had done.

"Thank you," Liberty said humbly.

"What are you doing here?" Abia asked.

"I'm just here as a guest this time," Liberty said, joking. "Nothing too major, just accompanying a friend."

"It is so good to see you. I thought I would never see you again."

Abia stared deeply into Liberty's eyes. She noticed something different: there wasn't any pain in those eyes. She had been in the business for more than twenty years, and she could sense pain by looking into a girl's soul. She knew that the eyes were windows to the soul, and she mastered how to read them. It made her warm inside to know that Liberty was out of the game and had found some type of peace.

"You're happy. I can see it all over your face. You are content where you are in life, right?" Abia said, hitting the nail directly on the head.

"Yes, I am." Liberty said proudly, impressed by Abia's words. "I just wanted to see you. You taught me a lot about life, and I will forever respect you for that. I just wanted to say thank you."

"No, thank *you*. Thank you for getting out of the lifestyle and getting to your happy. That's what life is about. That smile tells it all," Abia said proudly. She glanced back at the girls, knowing that she had to get back to them before the show started.

Liberty totally understood and quickly began backing toward the exit. "I know you are busy. I just wanted to say hello,"

"Look, please don't leave afterward. Let's talk and catch up," Abia said as she went back in the direction of the girls.

Liberty headed back to her seat, maneuvering through

the crowd. The place was noticeably more packed at that point, and the anticipation for the event was growing. She spotted Baron at the table, and he also saw her. He raised his hand to make sure she saw him amid the sea of people. When they locked eyes, Liberty smiled and waved at him. Liberty was anxious to tell him about seeing her old friend, but her smile was turned upside down when she saw Dahlia sitting a couple of yards away from Baron at a different table. Liberty stopped in her tracks, and her heart dropped to her stomach. Dahlia smiled and chatted with an unknown man, and Liberty instantly grew uncomfortable. Obviously, Dahlia didn't know Liberty was in attendance; she was much too comfortable, laughing and chitchatting. Liberty quickly tapped one of the waitresses and asked if she could borrow the mask that she wore. The waitress was reluctant to give up her mask, but she had been instructed that the main focus was to make everyone at the ball comfortable. So she agreed and pulled off her mask, which was decorated with feathers and rhinestones. It resembled masks from Mardi Gras. Liberty thanked the girl and quickly put on the mask, disguising herself. She made her way over to Baron, who was sitting at the table sipping a small glass of cognac.

"Wow, I almost didn't recognize you," he said as Liberty joined him at the table.

"That's the point. Listen, we have to talk," she said hurriedly, leaning in close to Baron. "The bitch I was telling you about . . . she's here." Liberty clenched her teeth.

"What?" Baron said, trying to understand why Liberty was acting so weird.

"Dahlia. She is here. She is behind us about three tables back." Liberty shot a quick glance, seeing Dahlia still talking with a man who sat at her table.

Liberty had broken down the whole story to Baron on the night he first reunited with her, so when he heard the name, he knew exactly who she was. He discreetly looked back and realized Liberty was talking about the same woman he had the rendezvous with in the restroom a couple of minutes ago. He chuckled to himself and focused back on Liberty.

"Ain't that a bitch?" he said under his breath, and he shook his head from side to side slowly. He smiled to himself as he thought about how he had almost fucked Liberty's archrival in the restroom. "Enough said. You want her dead?" Baron asked, straightforward, not even wanting to play with the situation. He hadn't gotten into any gangster shit in years, and honestly, it was getting his adrenaline pumping. He wanted to teach Liberty how to take care of a problem. He wanted to demonstrate how to nip a problem in the bud as soon as possible. Whenever an opportunity presented itself to end a beef, take it. That was his mindset.

"Absolutely," Liberty said. She wanted to end the feud for good, and this was the perfect time. They instantly began to brainstorm, and they put down a play that was legendary.

SEVENTEEN

DAHLIA HAD BEEN EYEING BARON MONTGOMERY ALL night. Jacob had disclosed more information about him, and she knew that she wanted to deal with him. He would be her next boy toy. Even though he was older, she planned to break him down and control him like a puppeteer. It was a new challenge, and she yearned for the domination. She had watched him talk to a waitress most of the night and wondered why he was so interested in the help and not her. Although she didn't know Baron, she felt offended.

In due time, I will be the only thing on his mind, she thought as she sipped on a glass of champagne. Jacob had made Baron sound even more enticing when he let Dahlia know about all of his accolades in the streets. *There is something about a powerful man*, she thought. Everybody in the room dreamed of doing business with Baron. His track record was impeccable, and he was known for good business.

The auction began, and the men watched as the beautiful, exotic women walked the stage, auctioning off their bodies. Men held up cards, signaling that they were interested in a girl onstage. Bids started at ten thousand and went up to one hundred thousand. Dahlia had been keeping an eye on Baron all night and noticed when he stood up and buttoned his suit jacket. He then headed toward the restroom, but not before looking at Dahlia and winking at her, as if he was saying, "I'm ready." Dahlia smiled as she accepted a drink from a passing waitress and took a sip.

I knew he would come around, she thought, and she felt a small tingle in her clitoris. She was ready to hook Baron, and she imagined riding his well-endowed dick reverse-cowboy-style in one of the restroom stalls. She swallowed the rest of her drink in one gulp and set the glass down. She then followed him toward the restroom. Every time she stepped, she felt her love box throb, and she couldn't make it to the restroom quickly enough. Baron looked back at her again before he walked into the ladies' restroom, and Dahlia knew that he meant business. It was about to go down.

Baron walked into the bathroom and immediately began to unzip his pants. He leaned on the sink, in the same spot Dahlia had earlier. He unzipped his pants and licked his lips, waiting for her. As soon as she walked in the door moments later, she began to pull down her panties.

"I knew you couldn't resist this blackberry," Dahlia said

as she pulled her dress up over her waist, exposing her neatly trimmed vagina.

Her juicy lips underneath were glazed, and her clitoris was so erect it slightly peeked out of her vaginal lips. She made her way over to Baron and immediately dropped to her knees. She pulled out his thick black pole and was pleasantly surprised by his thickness.

"Uhmm," she moaned in pleasure as she held his rising manhood close to her face, examining it. She was in love at first sight. She wrapped her lips around it, squeezed the base with one hand, and cupped his balls with the other. She quickly began to bop up and down his shaft, making slurping noises and humming as she gave him a performance he would never forget. Baron threw his head back in pleasure as he let Dahlia go to work. After a minute of oral sex, Dahlia began to get dizzy. She temporarily stopped and held her head back as her world began to spin. She put her hand on her head and frowned as she tried to figure out what was wrong with her. Baron slowly put his pole back in his pants and watched the scene unfold.

"What the fuck did you do to me?" Dahlia asked as she began to see stars.

"No, you did this to yourself," Baron said as he stepped away.

Dahlia lay down on the floor to try to regain her focus. Her vision was blurred, and the only thing she saw was the restroom door being opened. A pair of stilettos approached her. It was Liberty. Liberty had outsmarted her and was now standing over her.

Baron reached into his waistband and gave Liberty his gun. He had given her specific instructions. Handle Dahlia, walk straight out, and he would have the car waiting out front for her. "Don't mind the chaos or pandemonium. Just keep your cool and come straight out," he'd instructed. He knew that the gun blast would cause a scene, but because of the nature of the event, no cameras were on site, so they just had to leave, and it would be done. He gently grabbed Liberty's face and pecked her on the forehead. "Make it quick," he said, just before he headed out.

Liberty pulled off her Mardi Gras mask and looked down at Dahlia, who was slightly disoriented. The Xanax pills that Liberty had just gotten from Abia worked like a charm. She had slipped ten crushed-up pills into Dahlia's champagne, and Baron's plan was flawless. He predicted everything that would happen, and it did to the tee. Liberty pointed the gun down at Dahlia and began to remember all of the heartache that she had put her through.

"I thought I would never see you again. I wanted you out of my life for good. You always find your way to me. I am tired of this. You hurt me to the core! My own flesh and blood," Liberty said as anger took over her.

"Liberty?" Dahlia said as she looked up at her in confusion.

"Yeah, it's me. This will be the last day you ever will be in my life. This has to stop," Liberty said as she pressed the gun to the Dahlia's temple. She got ready to pull the trigger.

Dahlia closed her eyes and prepared for the blast. But Liberty couldn't do it. She was not an evil person, and she couldn't bring herself to pull the trigger. It was totally uncharacteristic of Liberty. She realized that if she went through with her actions, it would make her no better than Dahlia.

This isn't me, she thought as she lowered the gun and shook her head. She wasn't a killer, nor did she have a desire to be.

"Karma is going to do you worse than I ever could," Liberty said as she shook her head, disgusted. She headed to the door and heard Dahlia laugh.

"You should have killed me, bitch," Dahlia said bravely as she smiled and giggled to herself.

Liberty took a long, hard looked at Dahlia and smiled. "May God bless you. Karma is real. Trust. Karma is definitely real." Liberty walked out the door, leaving Dahlia alone in the restroom.

She did just as Baron instructed. She walked out the door, and as Baron promised, a car was waiting for her. Liberty never looked back; she never wanted to see Dahlia or her evil ways again. "I can't let her ruin my life again. I'm going to let karma catch back up with her," she whispered to herself.

Dahlia stumbled out of the back of the hotel, panting heavily, with her hand on her chest. She felt dizzy and could barely stand up straight. She felt nauseated, and she bent over, hurling vomit onto the pavement. She instantly began to feel better after relieving her body of the drug that she'd unknowingly ingested. Her heart pounded rapidly, and she knew that she had just danced with death. She knew that if that were any one of her other enemies, she would have a bullet in the back of her head. She was glad that it was Liberty, who didn't have the heart to pull the trigger. An involuntary smile spread across her face as she stood up and fixed her dress. She vowed to kill Liberty at a later time. *I'm going to murk that bitch, just for pointing a gun at me,* she thought, just before she let out a chuckle.

She reached into her cleavage and pulled out her cell phone. She was about to call Jacob to instruct him to meet her in the back alley with their driver so she could leave. Her vision was slightly blurred as she tried to look at the numbers on the phone, so she squinted her eyes and began to push the buttons. That's when she saw the headlights of a car coming down the alley. She noticed the black-tinted Escalade creeping. She smiled when she saw the car service's name on the front plate.

Jacob must have already called the car, she thought as she began to walk toward it. The truck stopped right in front of her, and she heard the sound of the doors being unlocked. Dahlia climbed into the backseat and began to tell Jacob what had just happened. She didn't even think to look at him—bad move. She looked at the driver and noticed that it wasn't the same driver she had earlier. She then noticed that someone was in the passenger side in all black with a ski mask on. She tried to scream, but the person next to her muffled her. It wasn't Jacob; in fact, it was a Caucasian man she had never seen in her life. The man placed a rag over her mouth, and Dahlia instantly realized that there was chloroform on it. She tried to fight back, but the man was extremely strong, and she was no competition. Dahlia began to black out, and within seconds, her whole world faded to black.

Baron headed to the airport and looked over at Liberty, who sat in the passenger seat. He understood the rules of the game and knew that he should have taken care of Dahlia. Liberty was no murderer, but he had to give her a chance to end her beef. He knew that she was playing with fire by not killing Dahlia. He had already made up his mind to handle it for her. He just wanted to make sure she was on the plane and safe. He had decided to kill Dahlia and go back into hiding across the border. He had no more business in the United States. He had found closure with his son through Liberty, and that was all he wanted. He had established more than enough connections for Liberty and had talked to old associates at the ball, and Liberty had an open line of credit for anything she needed. Baron pulled up to the airport and parked at the drop-off area.

"Go home, Liberty. I have a few things to take care here before I leave," he said. "I will be giving you a call soon with some contacts for you and your guys. Everything is taken care of."

Liberty nodded and leaned over to hug him. "Thank you. Thank you so much," she said as she gripped him tightly.

"No, thank *you*. Thank you, daughter." Baron unlocked their embrace and smiled at her.

Liberty returned the smile and got out of the car. Baron watched as she faded into the airport. He quickly threw the car into drive and headed back to the ball. He had to get back and find Dahlia.

Baron cruised through the L.A. streets in the rented Range Rover with his gun in his lap. He drove hastily en route back to the ball. Just as he was passing a crossway, a black truck pulled in front of him. *Boom!* He T-boned the other car. The loud sound of the collision echoed through the air. The two vehicles were the only ones on the road, and there were no witnesses in sight. Baron slammed on his brakes, causing his tires to burn rubber and leave skid marks on the pavement, but it was too late. His gun slid off his lap because of the sudden stop. Baron's airbag exploded, temporarily stunning him as the white balloon struck him in the chest and face. He took a second to compose himself and checked to see if he was OK. He had not been injured; he just was a tad discombobulated.

"What the fuck?" Baron yelled. He had braked just in time, and if he hadn't, he might have died. He breathed heavily and took a minute to calm himself. He stepped out of the car to make sure the other driver was OK. Just as he stepped fully out of the car, three black vans pulled up out of nowhere, boxing him in. He was being ambushed. The sliding doors of the vans popped open, and goons dressed in all black with automatic assault rifles hopped out. He was overmatched. Baron put both of his hands up in defeat.

"Fuck!" he yelled, knowing that he was helpless. He

instantly thought it was the feds, but he was wrong. There was nothing federal about the masked men, one of whom walked up to Baron and stuck a needle in his neck, injecting him with some type of serum. Immediately, Baron collapsed. The men quickly picked up his limp body and tossed him into the van.

EIGHTEEN

THE SOUNDS OF HEAVY BREATHING WERE THE only things to be heard in the room. Baron felt that he was bound to a chair and couldn't move his limbs. He slowly came to and felt as if he had been heavily drugged. The sounds of other people chatting became more coherent as he came to. He heard different voices all asking where they were. It was complete chaos as everyone tried to figure out what was going on.

"Where the fuck am I?" a female voice asked.

"I can't see anything! What's going on?" said a man.

"Whoever is behind this! Untie me right now!" said a man with a heavy Spanish accent.

"Please, help!" someone screamed.

This only confused and scared Baron even more. There was something over his head, and he saw nothing. It was absolute darkness. He tried to analyze the situation. He spoke, and his low baritone caused everyone to temporarily shut up.

"Listen! We can't figure this thing out if everyone is talking. So let's all relax and talk this out," Baron said calmly.

He tried once again to yank free from the chair, but it was to no avail. He came to grips with the fact that he wouldn't be able to free himself.

He took a deep breath and then continued to speak. "I was driving, and I got ambushed. Guys in masks jumped out on me, and then I remember everything going black," Baron said as everyone listened.

"That's exactly what happened to me, Baron," a female voice said as she also tried to release herself from the bondage.

Baron knew that the voice sounded familiar; he just couldn't put his finger on who it was.

"It's me, Anari," the woman said. Anari Simpson. The woman who could make it snow, heavy in Miami and a member of the Supreme Clientele drug syndicate. Baron was at a loss for words. There was definitely a connection between them. Now they needed to find out who else was in room.

"My name is Carter . . . Carter Jones," a man said. "The last thing I remember is waking up and seeing two masked men over me. I was in Spain, hiding. What the fuck is going on?"

"I'm Dahlia, and the last thing I remember . . ." Dahlia began to speak but was interrupted by the sound of a large door being opened.

Everyone froze, not knowing what to expect next. Some of the most controlling, powerful people were in that room, but ironically, none of them had control over what was about to occur. The sounds of shoes clicking on the floor echoed throughout the room. Every single soul in the room was on edge, and the anticipation was thick. It was as if they could hear one another's heartbeats. The clicks got louder and louder, and eventually they stopped.

The pillowcase was pulled from Baron's head, and the bright lights of the room amazed him. He looked around and saw that he was in a spacious room with marble floors. The artwork on the ceiling was elaborate, something like he had never seen before. The hand-painted ceilings were beautiful and high. Baron then looked at the huge, beautiful round oak table with a gloss that shone like no other. He sat at it, along with five other people who had pillowcases over their heads still. Baron was confused and amazed at the same time.

The man began to untie him, and Baron looked at the unfamiliar face and asked, "What's going on?"

The man freed Baron and smiled. "Hello, Baron. Please stay calm, for I will explain what is going on."

Baron rubbed his wrist and tried to relieve the discomfort in his joint from being tied up.

The tall, slender African American man began to untie the others, one by one. He was fair-skinned, with low-cut hair. He stood tall and had warm eyes.

"I apologize for having to bring you all here in this fashion, but it was the only way. Please do not be alarmed. I am not your enemy." The man had a smooth, relaxing voice. He spoke loudly and clearly; most of all, he spoke with confidence.

Once he uncovered everyone, there was complete silence. Everyone looked around the gigantic room and admired the black and white checkered floors and stunning paintings on the walls and ceiling. It was something none of them had ever seen before. It was simply amazing.

They all wanted to say something, but no one did. All that was heard was the slim man's voice and the sounds of everyone's movements. The slim man walked to the head of the table.

"Every single one of you has been handpicked. Every single one of you was specifically selected to help me and my organization achieve our goal. All of you are considered to be the best at moving narcotics, and we felt that you could help us move a new product." The man looked each one of the patrons in the eyes as he talked. He moved his hands elegantly as he spoke clearly. He grabbed everyone's attention, and they were itching to find out what all of this was for. He was about to tell them. "If anyone wants to walk out the door, you have the right. A car will be waiting outside and will take you to a private jet. That private jet will take you anywhere you want to go, and you will never hear from my people or me again. The choice is yours." He paused for a second and waited to see if anyone wanted to leave.

"Keep talking," Anari said as she clasped her hands. She set them on the table and leaned forward, obviously very interested in what the charming man had to offer.

"I agree. I want to hear more about this," Baron added.

Everyone seemed on the same page, so the man in front

gave a slight grin and continued. "My organization is a society that works together to achieve a common goal. As African American men, we have seen others do this on a massive scale and control the country. It's time to tip the scales and restore the order," he said with conviction. He placed both of his hands behind his back and slowly began to circle the table.

"My organization has created a drug that gets you as high as cocaine, and after the drug fades, it relaxes you like heroin. It is taken orally, and get this: it's not a health risk. There is no downside to the drug. It doesn't affect your health or your organs, or burn cells in the brain. A natural drug that gives you the high that you desire. It also gives you the libido and desire of a twenty-one-year-old student on spring break. All in one pill. Of course, we could take this public, but once the USDA gets a hold of it, the generic knockoffs would be on the streets in literally weeks. This would crumble our market and destroy our purpose. There is an exotic plant in India called the rebe flower. This particular flower is the only strand in the world, and we are the only ones who have access to it." The slim man stopped at the opposite end of the table.

"I want to take the time to introduce everyone here. To my left is Baron Montgomery. We've been looking for him for months now. He was one of the biggest drug distributors in the Midwest and is known for negotiations and business savvy.

"To the right of him is Carter Jones, head of the cartel

of Miami. Son of the late Carter Diamond. He is young and aggressive and has the leadership qualities that the youth flock to.

"Next we have the one and only Anari Simpson. I have to be honest with you, I am impressed. She single-handedly entered the ranks of the elite and is believed to be worth more than a billion dollars . . . street money."

"You betta believe it," Anari confirmed as she looked down at her manicured French tips cockily. The whole room burst into laughter and lightened up.

"I told you, she's a keeper," the slim man said, smiling and giving her a wink.

"Next we have Dahlia. Our African connect and our way to the five families in Africa. We want to use your connections to expand to your homeland."

Dahlia rolled her eyes and crossed her arms, not sold on the idea. "What can you do for me? Why do I need to help you? I'm doing just fine on my own. I have the African mob behind me. I am above this," she said, letting her greed and power trip take over.

"Like I said before, this is optional, and we are not begging you to be a part of this thing of ours. It was just an invitation," the slim man said calmly. "With all due respect, of course," he added, not wanting to offend anyone.

Dahlia looked across the table and saw the man who had set her up to be killed, just twenty-four hours before. She shot him a look that was deadly. If looks could kill, Baron would have been dead right where he sat.

"I'll pass. With respect, of course," Dahlia said sarcastically, and she slowly stood up. She was already planning how she would kill Baron for attempting to set her up.

"Well, thank you for your time, Dahlia. Sorry to have inconvenienced you with the sudden abduction. I wish you nothing but the best. The door is just to your rear." He politely waved his hand toward the exit door.

"I'll see you around, Baron," Dahlia said sarcastically as she looked at him with a menacing scowl. She then turned and headed out the door.

Baron knew she would be a problem, but he was more interested in what the man at the head of the table was proposing. He would handle Dahlia later. Baron liked what he was hearing and saw the bigger picture.

"Well, now that we have handled that, shall I continue?" the man asked. After getting nods from the group, he continued.

"Everyone, meet Millie," he said as he pointed to one of the two ladies in the room. "We have been watching her for years. Her game is heroin, and she has established a great track record in moving street product. We need that. We want to put this drug into high society in America but also on the street level.

"Last but not least, we have Brick. He has a following like no other." The slim man looked over at the well-built man, who remained quiet and observant. He had a real intense look, and his stature and strong facial features made him intimidating. "He owns the streets and has the muscle to handle whatever needs to be handled if a problem arises. His connections with the GDs and the Bloods will be instrumental. We need his followers to follow us. With that, we will be strong and have a street presence."

The room was quiet, and everyone looked at one another, trying to feel one another out. Most of the people had either done business together or heard about one another through the underworld's grapevine. So no formal introduction was needed. They all had one thing on common: they were successful drug dealers with power. They couldn't believe what was happening, but they all wanted in. One by one, each of them began smiling and slowly nodding, as if saying, "It's time to get money."

"Well, I guess there is nothing more to say. Anybody up for a trip?" the slim man asked as he rubbed his hands together, smiling.

"Absolutely," Anari said as she looked at him with her piercing eyes. "One more thing. Where are we? It's beautiful," she said, looking around at the gigantic room and its artwork.

"We are in Rome. This is inside the Vatican," the man said.

"You got to be kidding me," she said. She couldn't believe what she was hearing. They were talking business at the world's most religious place. This institution was more powerful than all of them combined. It was eerie.

"No lie. I will let you guys catch up and mingle. I will be outside waiting. Everyone has a car waiting for him or her outside. From here, we will go to the jet strip and head out. I will explain everything you need to know on the trip there.

"White people have been doing this for years. It's our turn. We don't even have to name this thing of ours; the public has already done that for us. Might as well accept and roll with it. Welcome to the Illuminati," the man said as he fixed his tie and cufflinks. He headed out of the room, leaving everyone in awe.

"What's your name, by the way?" Baron asked just before the slim man exited.

"Lazarus, but you can call me Ghost." he said smoothly, without even turning around. He disappeared into the darkness, leaving them alone.

"Lazarus?" Baron repeated with a frown. "From the Bible?" He had never heard such a peculiar name.

An hour later, they were all on a private jet, preparing to take off. Ghost was the last to board. The jet was by far the most luxurious aircraft that any one of them had ever been on. The plush interior was comfortable, and everyone sat around the small table in the middle of the floor. Ghost grabbed a bottle from the small fridge and began passing out glasses. He looked at the pilot and nodded. The sound of the propellers cranked, and Ghost began pouring everyone some of the bubbly.

"Here's to the new regime," he said as he raised his glass.

"To the new regime," everyone said in unison.

But just before they downed their drinks, Ghost leaned over and lifted the curtain so they could see outside. "I'm glad you all decided to get onboard. Because this was the alternative." He looked out the window. Everyone's eyes focused on the limo that was parked a few yards away from the jet. A man stepped out of the car while holding a woman who was beaten badly. He held her roughly by the back of the neck. As they looked closer, they saw that it was Dahlia. The man stood behind her and tossed her around like a rag doll as she cried in pain. Her lip bled, and both eyes were swollen. Ghost nodded, and the man pulled out a gun and sent two bullets through the back of her skull. Dahlia dropped, lifeless on contact. Those on the jet grimaced in disgust and turned their heads to avoid seeing the guts and brain matter splattered on the ground. Ghost closed the curtain and held his glass up. Karma was real. Dahlia's greed had led directly to her demise. In the end, she was her biggest enemy. Liberty did not have to pull the trigger on her, because Dahlia had destroyed herself.

"Welcome to the Illuminati," Ghost said, just before the jet took off and headed into the clouds.

It was the beginning of a new era.

EPILOGUE

RELIEF. LIBERTY WAS FLOODED WITH IT AS she emerged from the airport. After bidding farewell to Baron, she had quickly caught the first flight back home to Detroit. She felt as if all of the weight had been lifted from her shoulders. Finally, there was no looking over her shoulder, no fear, and no burden. Liberty had always stayed in her lane when it came to Dahlia. The pecking order had been established early on, and she never challenged it—until today. Now she realized that she was not the weak one. Just because she couldn't murder someone in cold blood or rule over an empire of men didn't make her weak.

Liberty had compassion, she possessed loyalty, and she had forgiveness in her heart. Liberty was twice the woman Dahlia would ever be, and she was proud of herself for ending that chapter in her life. Finally, the feud was over. She now had one last thing that she needed to handle before she could move forward.

She saw the white Cadillac pull up curbside as she exited the airport. The bite of the cold winter nipped at her skin through the thin fabric of the elegant dress. The temperature changed drastically from L.A. to Detroit, and she shivered as she walked through snow and ice to get to her ride. Rocko emerged from the driver's side and met her halfway, taking off his coat to wrap it around her shoulders. He opened the door and tucked her safely inside the warmth of his car before joining her inside. He pulled away from the airport smoothly. They rode in silence for a while, neither of them knowing what to say. It had been so long since they had been alone together. Since they'd fled L.A., Po was always the buffer between them. They had played nice, remained neutral, distant friends since the three of them had reunited, but as Liberty sat beside him, she knew that she wanted more. The racing of her heart was indication enough.

"Why did you call me, Liberty? Po would have scooped you from the airport," Rocko said.

Liberty fiddled with her fingers nervously. "I don't want Po."

Rocko scoffed and shook his head as he turned the steering wheel smoothly to the right to merge onto I-75. "You don't know what you want, ma."

"I want you, Rocko," she replied, her eyes large and honest.

Rocko was silent as he processed her words. He had tried his hardest to ignore his feelings for Liberty. He didn't want to be the snake nigga who got involved with his best friend's girl. Since coming to Detroit, he had acted so distant from Liberty that he sometimes came across as cold. It was all business between them, but here she was laying her feelings out in front of him. She was putting it all on the line.

"You know that can't happen, Liberty," he replied.

"I know you love me, Rocko. No matter how hard you try to hide it, no matter how much you force yourself to call me sis or treat me indifferently. I can see it in your eyes. It emanates off of you. I feel it even if you don't want me to," she whispered.

Rocko knew that he couldn't allow this to go further. He had to dead her feelings for him. No matter how much he wished that he would have met her first, he hadn't, and for them to be together would be wrong. It went against everything that he stood for as a man. His heart was begging him to accept her love. Rocko, a motherless child who was deficient in affection, needed her. He craved her like she was an addiction, but his mind was telling him no. His strong will was making him remain loyal to a friend who had already showed that he didn't deserve it. Rocko cleared his throat and opened his mouth to tell the biggest lie he had ever told.

"You're misreading things. If I haven't been clear, let me be now," he said. "I . . . do . . . not . . . want . . . you . . . Liberty." He was firm. His voice was cold and full of disgust, as if the possibility of him being attracted to her was preposterous.

Her mouth fell open in shock, and she blinked tears

away. It literally felt as if her heart had been torn in two. Her face turned red, and she felt her skin flush with heat. Embarrassed, she sat back and folded her arms across her chest. "Understood. Please, just take me home," she whispered as she looked out the window to avoid him seeing the tears that fell down her face.

Rocko heard the hurt in her voice, and he bit his inner cheek. He hated to be the one to cause her pain, Lord knew she had been through enough, but it wasn't his place to soothe her, either. *She's Po's girl*, he thought.

Finally, he pulled up to her home. He didn't even pull into her driveway. "Call Po the next time you need something, a'ight?"

Liberty didn't even look at him before she got out of the car and walked into her home.

As soon as she disappeared from sight, Rocko hit his steering wheel in frustration. He couldn't bring himself to pull away from her house. He had spoken the words to her, but when it came to reinforcing them with his actions, he was unable. He got out of the car and walked up to her door. With a heavy heart, he knocked.

She pulled open the door, her eyes filled with tears and her face wet with emotion.

"Come here, ma," he whispered. He pulled her to him, and their lips met. She melted into his embrace as he grasped the hair behind her ear and kissed her passionately. "I love you. Shit ain't right, but it's real."

"What about Po?" she asked.

"Yeah, Rocko, what about Po?"

Po's voice came from behind them, and both Rocko and Liberty turned around. They were caught red-handed, and neither of them had wanted Po to find out in this way. It made it look like betrayal when in actuality it was fate. There was an attraction between them that could no longer be denied. Fire burned in Po's eyes.

"Po, bro, I didn't want you to find out like this," Rocko started.

All Po saw was red. He swung, hitting Rocko across the jaw with a right hook.

"Po, stop!" Liberty screamed as the two men began to brawl.

In all of their years coming up together, they had never come to blows. It was always the beauty of a woman that divided men. Rocko sidestepped one of Po's lefts and then hit him with a powerful jab. Both men fought full force, as if they had always been enemies.

"Rocko, no! Po!"

Liberty's voice may as well have been a whisper, because it was no longer about her, it was about the win, about the pride of men. They soon tired, but neither of them would give up. Finally, Rocko tied Po up in a firm hold.

"Listen!" Rocko roared. "I'm going to let you go, but you gotta chill out, my nigga." He pushed Po off of him and nursed his nose, which he was certain Po had broken.

Liberty stood in between them, shaken and confused as she looked at them both.

"Let her choose," Po said as he sucked blood off of his busted lip and wiped sweat from his brow. His chest heaved as he caught his breath and glared at Rocko. "Who you rocking with, Liberty? Huh?"

Liberty could hear Po's anger, and she was filled with guilt.

"Don't think about us, ma," Rocko said. He could see her turmoil. It was written all over her face. "This is about you."

Liberty paused, and Rocko grew frustrated. *Love don't hesitate,* he thought. He shook his head and walked past her, right out of the house.

Po walked over to Liberty and pulled her into an embrace. "I forgive you, ma. Let's just start over. Fuck Rocko, fuck L.A., fuck the past."

Liberty pulled away from him. "Fuck you," she said. She headed for the door. Po grabbed her elbow, pulling her back to him. "You should have taken care of home when you had the chance. You fucked my family. You threw me away like trash. You can hate Rocko all you want, but he didn't take your girl, Po, you gave me away." She snatched her elbow away harshly. "Now, let go of my arm so I can go get my man."

Po's face fell in shock and disappointment as Liberty sprinted out the door.

"Rocko!" she shouted. "Rocko! Please, wait!" Rocko turned around, heated, eyes ablaze, but she didn't care. She jumped into his arms and kissed his lips. His hands cupped her behind as she wrapped her legs around his body. "I want you," she whispered.

Po came out onto the porch and shook his head in

disgust as he made his way to his car. When he reached the couple, he stopped to look Rocko in his eyes. The men squared off as Liberty clung to Rocko's shirt. The tension was thick, and Liberty didn't know what to expect next.

"Take care of her heart," Po said, his thoughts drifting to Scarlett.

"I plan to," Rocko replied.

Po smirked and retreated to his car before driving away.

Peace. It was something that had been so elusive to Liberty her entire life, but on this day, as she sat underneath the golden sun, she felt released—released from the fear, from the stress, from the chains that had bound her ever since she was stolen from her village all those years ago. She could feel the kisses as the heat from the rays kissed her light skin. It would undoubtedly leave a darkened tan. Her bare toes curled, squeezing the freshly cut grass as she lay on her back. Her delicate fingers gripped the pen as she thought of the note that she wanted to write. The white pages of her journal were filled with love quotes from her favorite authors and poets. Whenever she heard one that reminded her of A'shai, she wrote it down and then visited his resting place to leave a love note on his grave. Her fingers moved, writing in fancy cursive as she spoke the words aloud.

"Love is not love which alters when it alteration finds, or bends with the remover to remove: O no! it is an ever-fixed mark . . ."

It was from one of Shakespeare's sonnets. She tore the

paper from her book and folded it in half. She kissed it and placed it, along with a bouquet of flowers, on A'shai's grave.

"I miss you, Shai. I will never love anyone the way that I loved you. You can rest peacefully now. I'm safe, and I'm finally happy," she said. This visit was much different from her previous ones. She had finally accomplished what A'shai had always tried to give her. Freedom. She knew that he would be pleased. She stood to her feet, scooped up her small blanket and sandals. "I'll come here every year, A'shai, until the day we are reunited." She leaned over and kissed the cold brick, then turned to leave. The roundness of her belly caused her to waddle through the grass. She smiled when she saw Rocko pull out right on time. He parked on the dirt road of the cemetery, then got out of the Mercedes S-class to open her door. They were doing well. Liberty had given Rocko the connect that Baron had introduced her to at the Gentlemen's Ball a year ago. Rocko was slowly building an empire that spanned from Flint to Detroit. He was her provider, and as they got to know each other more every day, he was slowly becoming her very best friend. They hadn't heard from Po since the day she had chosen between them, and it was fine by them. Every relationship had a reason and a season. They had both concluded that Po had served as a bridge to bring the two of them together. Without Po, they would have never met, and now that they had, they no longer needed him around. All they wanted was each other.

"You have a good visit, ma?" he asked as he kissed her cheek.

She reached up and placed a hand on his cheek, and the stubble from his five o'clock shadow tickled her palm. She kissed him gently, and he instinctively placed a hand on her growing belly. "You are a good man," she whispered. She loved the fact that she didn't have to hide her love for A'shai from him. He understood her past, and he accepted it. He was unlike Po in so many ways. Po wasn't even half the man Rocko had turned out to be. He was her support. Rocko renewed her faith in love when she was sure that she would never find it again. Yes, she would always acknowledge A'shai as her first love, but she appreciated Rocko because he was her second great love, and he had been able to love her pain from previous relationships away. Liberty didn't want to fight her feelings for him any longer. She deserved a love like his. She realized that it wasn't her fault that she and Po hadn't worked out. He had given up on her. By thinking that the grass was greener with Dahlia, he left room for another man to make her happy; that man just happened to be Rocko. She was glad that Rocko was finally choosing love over loyalty. He had picked her, throwing all of the G codes he had learned coming up to the wind. He was living by his own rules.

"I'm good to you, Lib; everybody else don't see this side," he said with a crooked smile, one that she had grown to adore.

"Your secret's safe with me," she said playfully. She entered the car and waited as he walked around and slid into the driver's seat. He held one hand out for her, and she laced her fingers between his. He used his left hand to turn the wheel and steer the car out into traffic. She couldn't believe how her life had turned around. With the love of one man, she had been renewed. Now here she was, eight months pregnant and completely smitten. She had never expected Rocko to be the one she would end up with, but God had a way of showing her that her plans were not always the same as His. With Po, she always felt guilty, as if she had been trying to replace A'shai, but with Rocko, she felt she was exactly where she was supposed to be. He felt familiar, and in a lot of ways, he reminded her of A'shai. They were built the same. They both possessed a rare characteristic: loyalty. Liberty was addicted to a rare breed, and she was lucky to have found two in the same lifetime.

The light kicks of life thundered in her stomach. She had gotten used to the movements of her child as it grew inside of her. She shifted slightly in her seat as she felt another kick, this time much stronger than the one before. "Hmm," she moaned as she closed her eyes. There was a brief pain.

"Everything a'ight?" he asked.

Liberty sat upright in the car and gripped the side handle as another kick occurred. This time, the pain jolted her forward. "I don't know," she whispered. "I've never felt this pain before, and there is so much pressure."

"I'm not taking any chances. I'm heading to the hospital," Rocko stated, turning the car around immediately.

Liberty rubbed her stomach gently and tried to calm her baby. "No, I don't want to overexaggerate. I'm not due for another three weeks. This is probably just those Braxton

Hicks I told you about. My body is supposed to go through this. No need to panic over a false alarm."

"You know all that you're talking is just noise right now. We're going. I'd rather raise hell and have it be a false alarm than do nothing and risk everything," Rocko replied. "I dropped big money in that doctor's account. This is what we pay her for, to be there when we need her."

Rocko sped to the hospital and put the call in to their doctor to let her know they were on the way. By the time they arrived, Liberty could barely walk. Pain erupted through her abdomen. She was so distressed that tears clouded her vision. She had gone from calm to panicked because her body was telling her that this was not normal.

"This can't be happening," she whispered to herself as the fear of losing her child popped into her mind. This would be just fitting. She had never gotten to live the fairy-tale lifestyle for too long. Tragedy always struck her eventually.

"Rocko." She looked at him with anxious eyes.

"Don't worry, Lib. Everything is going to be OK. I feel it in my soul, ma," he said. He kissed the back of her hand and got out of the car. He ran into the hospital to retrieve a wheelchair and then gently moved Liberty. He rushed her inside.

Rocko tried his hardest to keep his cool. Liberty was unraveling by the minute, and he didn't want to lose his head and contribute to the chaos. If she was weak, then he had to be strong. He had to be levelheaded to support the woman he loved. He couldn't stop his heart from aching, however. On the inside, he was torn up as worry held possession of his insides. Rocko had never been emotional. In fact, until he met Liberty, he had never loved any woman, not even his own mother. Venturing into the territories of the heart was challenging for Rocko. It meant that he had to put someone before himself, and so far with Liberty, it had been worth it. All he wanted to do was put her first and protect her, but this was one thing that he had no control over. He couldn't bring their child into the world. That was her job, and he hoped that she was strong enough to pull it off. Liberty had a history of weakness, but right now, he needed her to find her inner strength. A small sense of relief flooded over him when he saw Dr. Blake. The tall, thin black woman wore a comforting smile as she stood in the middle of the hall waiting for their arrival.

"I've already registered you," she said. "Please follow me this way."

"I'm having a lot of pain," Liberty said. "Something just doesn't feel right."

The doctor placed a reassuring hand on Liberty's shoulder. "Don't worry. We'll find out what's wrong. I'm going to take good care of you and your baby, Liberty."

Rocko followed them into a room where he helped Liberty undress and slide into the hospital gown.

"Let's get you up in the stirrups," the doctor instructed calmly.

Liberty lay back and got into position, allowing the doctor to get a good view. Rocko stood near her head, holding her hand. He leaned over to kiss the top of her head, while silently fearing the worst.

"No wonder you're in a lot of pain, Liberty. You're dilating pretty quickly. Looks like you're going to have this baby tonight."

Suddenly, Liberty felt faint. She had survived so much in her lifetime, but she was unsure if she could survive this. She could feel Rocko's hand massaging her back. She saw the supportive looks from the nurses in the room. There were people all around her, encouraging her in this, but somehow she felt alone. She had no mother to hold her hand, no father to whisper words of reassurance. Liberty felt abandoned in that moment. Rocko's presence didn't seem to be enough to calm her fears.

"What are all these machines? Is everything OK? Is something wrong with the baby?" Liberty's questions were endless, and they were falling out of her mouth effortlessly. Nurses moved around her swiftly, moving Rocko to the side as they plugged IVs into her veins and put heart monitors on her stomach. She had so many tubes running through her body that she felt as if she might be dying.

"Answer her questions. We need to know what's going on every step," Rocko asserted.

"The machines allow us to monitor the baby's heartbeat. It's kind of low. If it drops any lower, I'm going to have to go in via cesarean," the doctor replied.

"A C-section? That means something is wrong with the baby," Liberty said in distress.

Rocko bent over her and kissed her lips. "I need you calm, our baby needs you calm. Breathe, ma. You had me in those Lamaze classes looking like a sucker. Now it's time to show what you learned," he joked. His charming smile caused her to smile, too. His spirit was infectious, and he began to breathe deeply in a pattern. She followed him. She felt Dr. Blake adjust the bed and lower the stirrups. She pulled the side rails up on the hospital bed, and suddenly, Liberty was being wheeled away.

"Rocko, let's get you sterilized. I don't like the way your baby's heartbeat is sounding. We're going into surgery now!"

Before Liberty could process anything, she was under a large glowing lamp, and everything around her was becoming hazy. She could hear voices that now sounded far away. The doctor barking orders. The machines around her blaring in distress. Rocko's voice demanding something.

There was so much pressure between her legs that it hurt. She could feel people pulling at her insides, and then she heard it—the sound of a baby's cry breaking through the air. Before she could enjoy the sweet sound of the melody, her entire world went black.

Liberty felt as if she were floating as she came out of her induced slumber. Her vision was blurry as she forced herself to open her eyes. She turned her head groggily, her head feeling like noodles, falling lazily against her pillow. She smiled when she saw her baby being held. She was about to call Rocko's name when suddenly, he turned around, and she saw the one face that she never thought she would see again. A'shai's. It was her long-lost love, standing across the room, carrying her newborn son. He rocked him lovingly in his arms.

"Hey, sleepy-head," he greeted her.

She was so groggy that all she could do was smile. "It's a boy, Liberty. He's perfect. You did good."

"Hmm," she moaned. She reached out to him, wanting to feel him, to touch him one more time. It had been so long. *This can't be real. This is a dream*, she thought. Even if it was, she didn't care; she wanted to live in this dream forever. It was the best dream she had ever had. He grabbed her hand as he cradled the baby in one arm. He stood over her, looking down at her lovingly. "I love you," she whispered. "I miss you so much."

"I love you, too. I'ma love you until I have no more air left in my lungs, Liberty. I'm so proud of you. You and me are forever, ma." He leaned down and kissed her forehead.

"Forever," she whispered as her eyes closed, savoring the moment. When she reopened them, it wasn't A'shai's face that she saw over her. It was Rocko's.

She looked left and then right, taken off guard and confused. *No*, she thought. *I wasn't done with him yet. I still had so much to say.* "Rocko?"

"Yeah, ma, it's me and our son," Rocko said.

Disappointment filled Liberty, but it quickly passed. Yes, she loved A'shai more than life itself, and she would miss him every day for the rest of her life. But he had come to her. She had waited for years, and his spirit had finally touched her. He loved her, he was proud of her, and he approved of her newfound family. Her seeing his face wasn't a mistake. It was his good-bye. It was what she had needed all along, and finally she felt closure. A'shai was finally resting in peace now that she had found happiness.

She reached out her arms and whispered, "Can I see him?"

"Of course you can. Liberty, meet our son," Rocko whispered as he passed their child to her.

An overwhelming amount of love blossomed in her heart when she laid eyes on his face. "He's so small," she whispered. "This is my child, our son."

She looked at Rocko, and he melted. He had never seen a woman look so beautiful. The affection that emanated off of her was unfiltered, and it was all reserved for his son. He had never had that. His mother had abandoned him as a small child, so the fact that Liberty loved his son made him love her that much more. If he hadn't been certain before, he was now. She was his angel, and although it had taken them forever to recognize their bond, he was grateful still.

Love danced all over Liberty's body, and she couldn't take her eyes off of her newborn. This was her son. Her purpose. She now realized that every single moment in her life had prepared her for this moment. Liberty had needed all of the pain she had endured to build character. She had to make all of the mistakes so that she could one day prevent the child she held from making them. Liberty's life was so clear in that moment, as she experienced pure love for the first time ever. Nothing compared to it, and as she brought her child's face to her lips, she felt joy.

"What do you want to name him?" she asked.

"King," Rocko replied.

"I love that," she whispered. "Hi, King," she sang, her lips stretched in a smile. She turned her head to Rocko and pursed her lips. "And I love you. Thank you for my fairy-tale ending."

Liberty had won. She had beaten all the odds. Through death, through prostitution, through human trafficking and family betrayal, she was still standing. Love had conquered all. Liberty was finally liberated.

READ MORE ABOUT ANARI, BARON, MILLIE,
and the rest of Ashley and JaQuavis's best characters in

ILLUMINATI: ROUNDTABLE OF BOSSES

(Coming APRIL 2014)

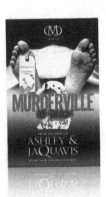

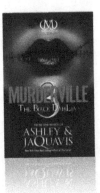

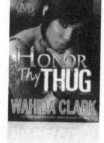

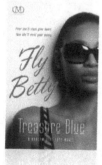